PRAISE

ORION
AND THE

"A FAST-PACED, RICHLY- highly regarded by (young a little blood and gore, and a protagonist who takes on and beats the bad guys."

— *Foreword Clarion* (5-star review)

"A GRAND ADVENTURE... The situations in which Orion finds himself are chilling enough to keep readers on the edge of their seats, but not scary enough to cause nightmares."

— *IndieReader* (5-star review)

"SUMMERHOUSE DELIVERS A ROUSING STORY filled with action and tense moments. Orion is subject to enough death-defying circumstances to lay low people twice his age, but most young readers should find it easy to suspend disbelief and enjoy the ride."

— *Publishers Weekly*

★ ★ ★ ★ ★

"A WILD, IMAGINATIVE ADVENTURE... Orion is a smart, fun-loving boy whose bravery and humor mark him a timeless hero alongside Huckleberry Finn. Recommended for any young reader who loves adventure."

— *Kirkus*

★ ★ ★ ★ ★

"A GRIPPING ADVENTURE/FANTASY TALE for young readers ages 9 and older. Even the most reluctant young reader will find this saga promises an energetic, vivid read."

— *Midwest Book Review*

"A FANTASTIC, FAST-PACED, AND CHARMING ADVENTURE... If you are a parent looking for a good adventure novel for your child, look no further."

— *RisingShadow* (5-star review)

"THE STORYTELLING FEELS TIMELESS... a true page-turner."

— *The Children's Book Review*

"THE BEST CHILDREN'S FANTASY I've read in a long time."

— *Bookworm for Kids*

"A RIPPING YARN... a wild, roller coaster adventure ride."

— *Amazon Top 500 Reviewer*

"SURE TO PLEASE children ages 8 and up."

— *Mr. Tierney's Library*

ORION POE
AND THE LOST EXPLORER

BY

WILL SUMMERHOUSE

SHAKE-A-LEG PRESS

THE AUTHOR GIVES SPECIAL THANKS to his editor, Robin Cruise of Red Pencil Consulting, whose sharp pencil and even sharper eye made this book a far sight better than it otherwise would have been.

Orion Poe and the Lost Explorer
Text © 2014 by Will Summerhouse
Cover illustration by Pritesh Rane © 2014 by Pritesh Rane

Library of Congress Cataloging-in-Publication Data
Summerhouse, Will
Orion Poe and the Lost Explorer / by Will Summerhouse. 1st ed.
p. cm. — (The Amazing Adventures of Orion Poe, Book One)

Summary: Orion Poe joins an expedition to the Arctic to search for a lost explorer. But once there events take an unexpected turn, and to survive he must outwit a scheming treasure hunter, team up with a gang of thieves, and take on a tyrant with an anger management problem.

[1. Action and Adventure—Juvenile Fiction. 2. Mystery—Juvenile Fiction. 3. Explorers and Exploring—Juvenile Fiction. 4. Franklin, Sir John, 1786–1847—History—19th Century. 5. Lost explorers—History. 6. Steampunk—Juvenile Fiction.]

ISBN 978-0-9860614-0-0

Library of Congress Control Number: 2013951553

Published in Seattle, Washington

CONTENTS

IN MEMORY OF MY GRAMPA, PATRICK

who took me hunting in the woods of Maine
when I was just three years old, and let me drive
his pickup truck across a bridge.

CHAPTER 1

THE MAN WITH THE
PURPLE NOSE

IF you saw the news reports about my adventure at the top of the world, you didn't get the whole story. I don't know why, but they left out the best parts, like how I got chased all over the place, and shot at, and knocked out, and almost eaten. On top of that they skipped over the beginning. My grampa said it just shows that if you want something done right you have to do it yourself. So I figured I'd tell the story myself—all of it, exactly the way it happened. And to do it right I have to go back to the night of the storm.

This storm wasn't one of your regular nor'easters like we get up here in Maine sometimes, but more like a hurricane. Toward evening the sky clouded over and began to darken up, and the sea took on an angry kind of look. Then all at once everything went dead quiet; even the crickets stopped chirping. Not long after that there was a strange noise off in the distance, like a ghost wailing. It got louder and louder, until I didn't think it *could* get any louder—and then a wall of wind slammed into the house so hard it tore the satellite dish right off the roof. The next minute here comes the rain, pouring down in sheets.

My grampa threw on his slicker and went next door to the lighthouse to start up the beacon. When he got back he said, "Looks like a real apple-shaker. Better stay in tonight."

So we stayed in. With the satellite dish gone we couldn't watch any television, so my grampa drank a bottle of wine and fell asleep in his favorite chair while I tried to read the book that Dell Robbins had lent me when school let out for the summer—the one about the boy who's half god and his friend who's half goat. But it made me sleepy, so I turned off the lights and pulled my chair up to the window, and sat in the dark and watched the storm. The wind was howling, and the rain lashed the window; then—BOOM!—a big roller would crash into the bluff, and after that a real screamer of a gust would come along and shake the whole house. It was so dark I couldn't see anything, except when the lighthouse beacon swept across the sea—and then I'd get a glimpse of complete chaos: waves as tall as mountains, with their tops ripped clean away by the wind and their faces streaked with foam, pitching and plunging and tossing every which way, and stacked up one behind the other as far as I could see. I never saw anything like it.

Well, about half an hour ran by—and all along the storm getting wilder and wilder—when suddenly the light flashed across something among the waves. Before I could make out what it was, the light passed on. So I waited for it to swing around again, and—there! A boat, with a man at the tiller! It was hurtling down the face of a giant wave and heading straight for the rocks at the mouth of the cove. I didn't lose another second staring at it, but jumped up and ran to wake my grampa. I shook him hard and said, "Grampa, wake up, wake up!"; but dang it all, he wouldn't rouse up! So I threw on my slicker, and grabbed the flashlight and set out for the cove on my own. The rain stung my face and streamed down my neck, and the wind tore at me so hard I had to fight not to get blown off my feet. I made my way along the path at the top of the bluff, to the old stump, and then dropped down through the woods to the cove. But when I got onto the beach and saw how monstrous high the waves were, and how they were tumbling over and thundering down on the sand, I pretty much gave up hope of finding anyone alive. I just couldn't see how a boat could land in surf like that and not get smashed to pieces.

So I was more than a little surprised when I got halfway down the beach and discovered a boat that wasn't smashed to pieces. She was about sixteen feet long and had the name *Lady Jane* painted on her bow in gold letters; later I found out that she was what they call a "jolly" boat. The surf had flipped her upside down and thrown her all the way up to the driftwood line.

CHAPTER 1

I got down on my belly and shined the light under her, but there was nobody there. I looked among the driftwood next, and poked through the wreckage that was scattered all around; nobody there, either. Then I hunted along the tree line, and all up and down the beach and among the rocks at both ends; nothing. The sea must've got him, I thought.

So I started for home, feeling a bit sorrowful for the man even though I didn't know him from a bar of soap. Well, I hadn't gone far when I hooked my foot on something and fell flat on my face. When I shined my flashlight back to see what I'd tripped on, what do I see poking out from between two driftwood logs but a pair of legs! It scared the pants off me at first; but then I noticed that the legs were attached to a man, and I was all right again.

I never saw a dead person before, and I didn't really want to see one, either. But I couldn't just leave him there without first making sure that he *was* dead. So I took a deep breath, and climbed onto the driftwood and shined the light on his face. And what a face it was! Just wild. It was covered with freckles and badly windburned. His lips were blistered and cracked, and his nose was purple—not your regular purple, but an ashy-brown kind of purple, like a rotten eggplant, or dried fish guts. His hair was long and tangled, and as red as a lobster; so was his beard. I could tell right away he wasn't dead, because there weren't any crabs on him. If he'd been dead they would've already been having him for supper.

I climbed down and pulled him out. He had a nasty gash on his leg and some smaller cuts and bruises, but other than that he looked all right. At least he was breathing, anyway.

I had to get him home somehow, but at first I couldn't see any way to do it. Then I hit on an idea. I found a couple of oars in the wreckage, along with some rope and a small sail, and made a rough stretcher. I rolled him onto it and lashed him down so he wouldn't slide off, and then I started back up the beach, dragging him behind me. The house was only half a mile away, but what with the wind, and the rain, and the man being so heavy and all, it took me a good hour to get him there, and by the time I set him down in the front room I was ready to drop.

My grampa had gone off to bed by then, so I went up to his room and gave him a good shake. He woke up this time, looking all bleary-eyed, and wanted to know what the matter was. I told him I'd found a man with a purple nose on the beach. He didn't believe me; he said I had a nightmare was all, and to go back to bed. I said it wasn't a nightmare, and if he didn't believe me he could go downstairs and see for himself. So he said all right, he *would* go. Then he heaved himself out of bed, grumbling about how this had better not be another one of my shenanigans, and followed me down. And wasn't he surprised when he saw the man!

"You think he's a lobsterman?" I said.

"Do lobstermen wear clothes like that?" he said. "Look at 'em: they're as white as snow."

He was right; under all that dirt and sand and blood they *were* as white as snow. And even stranger, when the light hit them they sparkled a little. I hadn't noticed it before.

That wasn't the only strange thing. He was wearing one of those little silver heart-shaped lockets that girls sometimes like to wear, and when we opened it we found a picture of him with a lady and a little girl inside. This girl was around seven or eight, and had freckles and red hair; the lady had black hair. They were dressed in old-fashioned clothes, like people sometimes get their pictures taken in at carnivals and state fairs and such. On top of that, when we peeled off his clothes we found three monstrous scars running clear across his back. It looked to me like somebody had whipped him, but my grampa said no whip would leave scars that deep. As for his purple nose, my grampa thought that was caused by frostbite—only it beat us both how anybody could get their nose frostbitten in the middle of summer.

We put him on the spare cot, then I went upstairs and got a blanket while my grampa cleaned the gash in his leg and put a bandage on it. After we got him tucked in I asked my grampa if he thought the man was going to be all right.

"Should be," he said, "as long as he stays off that leg for a few days. If he doesn't, it might get infected."

Not long after that I went up to bed. I was beat, but for the longest time I just lay there, staring into the dark and wondering about the strange man downstairs. I imagined all kinds of ways to explain his frostbitten nose and those awful scars on his back—and some of them were pretty wild. But as I would soon find out, nothing I imagined was anywhere near as strange and fantastic as the truth.

"THE TERROR! THE TERROR!"

THE storm blew itself out during the night, and by the next morning the world looked bright and clean, like it had been scrubbed. When I went downstairs the man with the purple nose was still asleep, so me and my grampa ate breakfast by ourselves. We were just finishing when we heard a crash in the front room. We both jumped up and ran to see what it was about, and when we got there we found him stretched out on the floor, with his legs tangled up in the blanket and his face as gray as ash.

We put him back on the cot, and then my grampa mixed some salt and sugar in a jug of water and told him to drink it. He drained the whole jug in one go. After that he stared at us, looking puzzled. Finally he says, "Where am I?"

"This is the West Quoddy Head lighthouse station," said

my grampa. "I'm Patrick Poe, the keeper. And this here's my grandson, Orion."

He only looked more puzzled than before.

"You got a name, fellah?" said my grampa.

"Name? I—I— Yes. It's Collins."

"Well, Mr. Collins, you're mighty lucky to be alive."

"How did I get here?"

"You can thank Orion for that. He found you wrecked in the cove last night and brought you up here."

But Collins didn't thank me; he just gave me a suspicious kind of look and asked me if I'd found anything with him.

"You mean besides the wreckage from your boat?" I said.

"Yes," he said. "Something personal."

I said no, I didn't remember seeing anything like that. He looked worried, then, and said, "How far away is the cove?"

"About half a mile," I said.

"Will you take me there?"

"What, *now*?"

"Yes. Hand me my clothes." And he started to sit up.

"Now hold on there, fellah," said my grampa. "You're in no shape to be going to the cove or anywhere else right now. You need to stay off that leg for a few days and let it heal up. You're welcome to stay here if you like, or we can drive you home. Whereabouts do you live?"

"You don't understand," said Collins. "I had something with me—something important. I've got to find it."

"Well, that's easy enough. You just tell us what it is, and Orion here will run down to the cove and look for it."

But he wouldn't tell us what it was, and when my grampa wanted to know why not he just clammed up and refused to say another word. So my grampa got mad, and gave him his clothes and said, "Suit yourself, mister. If that leg of yours gets infected, it won't be nobody's fault but your own."

"Hang my leg!" said Collins. "I don't give a fig about my bloody leg. Don't you see? I've got to find it before—"

He broke off all of a sudden and stared at us with a look that reminded me of a hunted animal; then he pulled on his clothes and struggled up to his feet. At first he put all of his weight on his good leg; but when he tried to shift some of it onto the bad one his face went all ashy again, and he had to grab my shoulder to keep from falling over. You could see he was in awful pain. But he just gritted his teeth and said, "So what'll it be, Mr. Poe? Will you let your grandson show me the way to the cove, or do I have to find it myself?"

My grampa never could stay mad for long, and when he saw how much Collins wanted to go to the cove he eased up and said I could take him. So Collins leaned on my shoulder and we started out for the cove. We had to stop every now and again so he could catch his breath, and when we got to the old stump he had to sit down and rest for a while. But at last we got to the cove, where we found the jolly boat just as I'd left her, upside down near the driftwood line. Collins wanted to crawl up under her and look for whatever it was he was so anxious to find, but he was too big to fit under the gunwale; and besides, with his hurt leg he couldn't have done it anyway. So he asked me if I'd do it for him. I said I would, and asked what he wanted me to look for. "A white knapsack," he said.

So I got down on my belly and slithered underneath the jolly boat. It was so dark I couldn't see a thing; but then as my eyes got used to the gloom I began to make things out. I found a small cask with some foul-smelling water in it, and a busted compass in a little wooden box, and a lead ball the size of a marble, and an old clasp knife with the tip broken off, and an empty tin box and other things like that. But I didn't find a knapsack, so I slithered back out and told him it wasn't there. He asked me if I was sure, and when I said I was he started to hop around among the wreckage, hunting for the knapsack. I felt sorry for him, so I helped.

There were torn sails and broken spars and other kinds of wreckage scattered all over the place, so we searched through that first; then we hunted up and down the beach and along the driftwood line. We looked everywhere, but we couldn't find it. Where could the stupid thing be, I wondered? Then I glanced over at the woods. Could the surf have thrown it clear into the trees? There was only one way to find out, so I went and looked. Sure enough, when I got to the tree line I spotted a white knapsack dangling from a branch high off the ground. I climbed up and got it.

Collins looked ever so relieved to have his knapsack back; he said he was greatly obliged to me, and that I'd just saved a life. I thought he meant *his* life, somehow, but I couldn't quite make out how, and before I could ask him about it he leaned on my shoulder and said he was ready to go back.

I figured he'd stay off his feet now and build his strength up, but as it turned out I was wrong about that. Every day, up until the end, he would get up before dawn and go out to the bluff with a spyglass under one arm and a crutch he made from an old shovel my grampa let him have under the other. All day long he would hop from the lighthouse to the stump and back, stopping every now and again to scan the sea with his spyglass, and he never came back to the house until after the sun went down. I asked him one day what he was looking for, but he wouldn't say. He didn't say much, generally, except when he absolutely had to, and then just a word or two. And if I ever asked him where he came from, or how his nose got frostbitten, or what made those horrible scars on his back, he'd just flash his eyes at me, and look so fierce I'd wish I was someplace else.

He was mysterious in other ways, too. When my grampa phoned the Coast Guard station at Eastport they told him they hadn't had any reports of anyone named Collins being missing at sea. And then there was his leg. My grampa tried to tell him that if he didn't stay off it and rest up his wound might get infected, but he wouldn't listen, and he wouldn't let my grampa change his bandage, either. So after a couple of days my grampa stopped bothering about it.

As for the knapsack, he never let it out of his sight and he never let us see what was inside it. Every night after he came in from the bluff he would take a clean sheet of paper and a pencil out of it when he thought I wasn't looking, and sit in the corner and draw. If he ever caught me trying to peek at the drawing he'd whip it out of sight, and he wouldn't draw again that night. He was always jittery, too. If he heard even the slightest noise outside he'd jump up from his chair, and switch off the lights and peep out from behind the curtains. My grampa thought he had a loose screw, but it seemed to me there might be more to it than that.

But worst of all was his nightmares. Every night he would jolt us awake with a horrible shriek, and then we'd hear him thrashing around on the cot and wailing, "The Terror! The Terror!" until my grampa went downstairs and woke him up. After that I'd lie awake, wondering what "the Terror" could be, until at last I'd drift off into my own nightmare about it. Sometimes it would be a cold black fog, swirling around my legs and trying to suck me down into it; other times it was a creature with empty eye sockets and no mouth, running and leaping and chasing after me along the bluff, or grabbing at my legs as I tried to scramble up the face of the cliff. It was a wonder I didn't wake up screaming myself.

One morning, after an especially rough night, I asked my grampa what he thought "the Terror" was.

"I haven't got the foggiest idea," he said. "But I'll tell you this: a man doesn't have nightmares like those unless something horrible has happened to him."

"Like how horrible?" I said.

"Like as horrible as it gets."

THE PHANTOM SHIP

SO five or six days passed by, until one evening, while I was heading home after exploring in the woods all day with Dell Robbins and the rest of the boys, I happened to look out across the water and saw a tall ship. She was painted white from stem to stern and had a flag with a bear and a wolf on it. There was a bank of heavy fog rolling in from the sea just then, and I watched her ghost along the edge of it until the fog rolled over her and swallowed her up.

I was curious, naturally; I'd never seen a tall ship like that before, and I didn't know what to make of it. I decided I'd go ask my grampa about it, but then I remembered that he had driven down to Bangor to pick up the new satellite dish and wouldn't be home until late. So I figured I'd ask Collins instead; I was pretty sure *he'd* seen it. But when I got out to the bluff he wasn't there. That's odd, I thought; he's always out here in the daytime. Maybe he went back to the house to get something. So I went to look, and sure enough, that's where I found him. He was asleep in his chair, with his chin resting on his chest and his long hair hanging down over his face. And on his lap there was a bunch of drawings.

Now I'd been wondering about those drawings ever since I first saw him making them, and when I noticed them just sitting there like that, and him being asleep and all—well, I figured he wouldn't mind if I had a peek. So I slipped them off his lap and flipped through them. There were seventeen altogether, and every one showed the same thing: a tall ship sailing over a stormy sea, with an iceberg in the background. Then I noticed something that gave me a real jolt—the ship was flying a flag with a bear and a wolf on it! I forgot I was trying to be quiet, and I blurted out, "That's funny!"

"What is?" said a voice.

I almost jumped out of my shoes. When I looked up there was Collins, staring out at me from behind his long tangled hair. His eyes were dull and glassy, and his face was the most awful white—not the pale white of someone who's fainted, but a dead white; a waxy, bleached-out white, like a corpse. It had little red blotches all over it, too; so did his hands.

"Are you all right, Mr. Collins?" I said.

"What's funny?" he said. "What did you mean?"

"Oh, nothing. It's just that I saw a ship that looks like the one in your drawings."

His eyes went wide, and he stared at me like a wild man.

Then he grabbed my arms—which startled me half to death, being so sudden and all—and said, "When?!"

"Just now," I said. "Why? What's the matter?"

"Devil take her! I've got to think." He let go of me, and thought. Then he said, "Was she heading for the cove?"

"I think so. Why?"

"I've been such a bloody fool! Why didn't I burn the jolly boat days ago? Wait—I may still have enough time to hide it. Quick, hand me the knapsack."

I did it. He got out a little flask and took a swig from it. In a minute the color came flooding back into his face, and his eyes got some of their old fire back. He put the flask in his pocket and said, "I have to hide the jolly boat, but I'm not sure if I can do it on my own. Will you help me?"

I said I would, even though none of it made any sense.

"Good lad. Let's go. No, wait! I forgot something."

He dug into the knapsack again, and this time out comes a pistol. It was one of those old-fashioned ones like you see in history books, with a stubby barrel and flintlock. Before I could ask him why he needed it he shoved it under his belt and went hopping out the front door on his crutch, calling over his shoulder for me to hurry. I ran after him.

By the time we got down to the cove his face was starting to look pale and blotchy again. He was breathing hard, too, so he sat down on a log and told me to get started while he caught his breath. I began gathering up pieces of driftwood and tossing them on top of the *Lady Jane*. After a minute he said, "No, Orion, not like that. Here, let me show you."

He got up and was about to take a step toward me when all of a sudden his eyes rolled back, and he let out a groan and toppled over like a tree. He hit the ground so hard the pistol shot out from his belt and went skittering under the jolly boat. I ran over to him and rolled him onto his back; his eyes looked like a couple of misty marbles. I gave him a good shake and said, "Mr. Collins! Are you all right?" He blinked a few times and stared at me; he looked puzzled, like he was trying to make out who I was. Then a little smile came into his face, and he said, "Ah, Dr. Little! Is that really you?"

I didn't know anybody named Dr. Little.

"No," I said. "It's just me, Orion."

I might as well have said I was Captain America, because he just called me Dr. Little again, and said how glad he was to see me. He wanted to know why I hadn't come sooner, and where was my doctor's bag, and was somebody named Rosie all right. Then he launched into the wildest kind of talk—something about a laughing devil, and a creature with fiery eyes, and a secret door underneath a tomb, and a river that ran under the earth. But mostly he talked about a place he called the Devil's Graveyard—and some of the things he said about it made my blood run cold.

Then he grabbed my hand and said, "We've got to hide the *Lady Jane*, Doctor. The Terror is coming! Do you hear me? The Terror is coming!"

You can bet I didn't like hearing that! My own nightmares about "the Terror" came rushing back to me, and I wanted to hightail it up to the house and lock all the windows and doors. Only I couldn't leave Collins there; I had to get him back to the house somehow. But how, I wondered? Then I remembered the flask. I got it out of his pocket, and put it up to his lips and said, "Here, drink some of this."

"What is it, Doctor?" he said.

"It's, uh—medicine. It'll fix you right up."

He said all right. I wasn't sure how much to give him, so I poured the whole flask down his throat. He sputtered and coughed till the tears ran down his cheeks; then here comes the color flooding back into his face again. His strength came back, too, and he seemed to know who I was now. I wanted to get him home before it wore off, so I didn't say anything about the boat not being hidden but just shoved his crutch under his arm and hustled him off.

By the time I got him back up to the house the sun had dropped behind the trees, and the fog had rolled over the top of the bluff and was creeping along the ground toward the lighthouse. I helped him onto the cot, then ran around and locked all the windows and doors. After that I went into the kitchen and called my grampa. He was in his truck, driving back from Bangor. I told him all about the red blotches on Collins's skin, and how he passed out at the cove and talked wild. My grampa said his wound must've become infected and he most likely had blood poisoning. He got mad, then, and called Collins a chowderhead for not listening to him. After that he said he'd send help, and hung up.

When I checked on Collins his face looked blotchy again. "What happened?" he said. "Why were we at the cove?"

"You wanted to hide the *Lady Jane*, remember?" I said.

"Oh, yes. I remember now—the Terror is coming!"

I did wish he'd quit with that Terror business! It gave me the heebie-jeebies. He was quiet after that; I could see he was thinking. Finally he looked up.

"Listen, Orion," he said. "It's no longer safe for you here. I want you to take my knapsack and go hide in the woods until it's over."

"Until what's over?" I said.

"There's not enough time to explain—just take it and go. After I'm gone give it to your grandfather. It has something important in it. He'll know what to do with it."

"But I can't just leave you!"

"Don't worry about me. If I get half a chance, I'll take that devil with me."

Before I could ask *what* devil he reached for his pistol—and when he didn't find it he said, "My pistol! Where is it?"

"You dropped it at the cove," I said.

"Curse this bad luck! First my leg gets infected, and now I lose my bloody pistol. Is there no end?"

He still wanted me to take his knapsack and go hide out in the woods, but I couldn't just leave him like that. I didn't know what "the Terror" was, or if it was even real. But the white ship was something else; I'd seen it with my own eyes, and if there really was somebody—or something—aboard it that wanted to kill him, how could I run away and leave him there without anything to defend himself with?

I couldn't, that's how.

So I threw around for an idea. My grampa had a hunting rifle he kept in a trunk in the attic, but the trunk was locked and I didn't know where he kept the key. What about my baseball bat? No. Then it hit me—the pistol! I'll just scoot back down to the cove and get it.

The next thing I knew I was running out the front door. Collins called after me to come back, but I pretended not to hear him. It was almost dark now, and the fog had made it to the lighthouse and was beginning to curl around it. Well, what with the darkness, and the fog, and the frightful scare that Collins had put into me about "the Terror" and all, I suddenly got a bad case of the jitters, and as I ran past the old stump and plunged into the woods I couldn't shake the feeling that something terrible was about to happen.

CHAPTER 4

WHAT HAPPENED AT THE COVE

I didn't slow down until I reached the cove. The fog was so thick I couldn't see the water, and except for the sound of the waves lapping on the beach it was as still and quiet as a graveyard; a little too quiet, it seemed to me. But I couldn't chicken out now and go back empty-handed—no, I had to get that pistol, no matter what. So I worked up my courage and started down the beach.

I hadn't gone far when a noise came out of the fog—or I thought one did, anyway; I was so jumpy I couldn't be sure. I stopped and listened, but all I heard was the water lapping on the beach. Then—there it is again! A creak, like someone had stepped on a loose floorboard. The next minute a voice sang out, "By the mark, six fathoms!" Another voice barked, "Silence on deck, there!" It was quiet again after that—only

I could hear my heart knocking against my ribs. Then there was a splash and a rattling noise that sounded like an anchor chain running out. I stood there, frozen to the spot; I was too scared to go on, and too curious to turn back. The sound of a boat being lowered into the water jolted me out of it, and in another second I was running for the *Lady Jane* as fast as I could clip it. I didn't slow down until I got to her.

Now for the pistol! I dropped to the ground, and reached under the gunwale and groped around for it. But I couldn't find the stupid thing. I was beginning to worry that I might be taking too long when I heard a noise that made my heart stop; it was that crunching kind of noise a boat makes when it lands on a beach. I thought about bolting for the trees, but decided I couldn't risk it; they might see me, whoever "they" were. So I scrambled back to the stern, where the gap under the gunwale was wider, and slid under the jolly boat as quick as I could. Then I peeped out through the gap on the other side—and tried to remember to breathe.

Pretty soon here come seven or eight men trooping up out of the fog, looking like smoky ghosts. They were all wearing the same kind of sparkly white clothes as Collins wore, and they had muskets slung over their shoulders—real ones, like you see in museums. The man who was leading them had a pistol like the one Collins had tucked under his belt, and he wore a helmet shaped like a bell. He was a real bulldog of a man, short and thick, with a pug nose and small, ugly eyes set too close together. I would've bet my whole collection of superhero trading cards that he wasn't friendly.

"Look, sir!" one of them said. "A boat!"

They hurried up to the jolly boat and began throwing the driftwood off her. A voice said, "It's her, Colonel—the *Lady Jane*!" Another voice—I didn't need anybody to tell me that it belonged to the man with the helmet—growled and said, "Out of my way, you infernal curs! By God, so it is!"

"Should we turn her over, sir?" somebody said.

You bet a scare shot through me then! But the man with the helmet—the one they called Colonel—he said, "Don't be a muppet, Downing. Collins isn't hiding under there. He could never fit under the gunwale." Then he barked, "You there, Gibson, take those three men and return to the ship. Give my compliments to His Lordship and inform him that I've found the *Lady Jane*. You two stay here and watch this boat. And look sharp—Collins may be close by. Fowler, you come with me."

So Gibson and three other men went back the way they'd come, while the colonel trotted away in the other direction with Fowler. The two men who were left to guard the boat leaned their muskets against it and sat down on the hull right above my head; they were so close I could've reached out and touched their heels if I'd wanted to. But I didn't want to.

I heard a match being struck, then got a whiff of tobacco. After a minute one of them says, "Well?"

"Well what, Joe?" says the other.

"Well fork it over, Harry. That's what."

"Fork what over?"

"Why, the ten shillings you owe me, you shifty dog."

"Ah, now, Joe, ain't you countin' your eggs before they're in the puddin'? We haven't found Collins yet. And until we do, I don't owe you spit."

"You heard the colonel. He said he's close by."

"How does the colonel know? He said that back when we was in the Devil's Graveyard, and did we catch him then? I say he's long gone by now."

"And I say stow your prevaricatin' and pay up."

"Ah, there's another one of your highfalutin words. Greek, is it? You always did talk high, for a carpenter's mate."

"So I am, too! And proud of it."

"Keep your bloody voice down, you clod! Do you want to bring the colonel down on our heads?"

"My father was a carpenter's mate," Joe grumbled.

"And a good one, too," said Harry, "when he wasn't too drunk to hit a nail on the head."

"Why, you snivelin' lubber!"

There was a WHACK!, and they fell to the ground fighting.

I'd been so interested in what they were saying that I had forgotten about the danger I was in. Now I remembered it, and I decided I'd better clear out of there before the others came back. So I began to crawl out the other side. Then my arm brushed up against something—the pistol! I shoved it in my belt, then slid the rest of the way out and busted for the trees, with my heart going like gangbusters. I expected to hear a musket bang out and get a bullet in the back, but I made it to the woods all right and jumped behind a tree. When I peeped back out they were still going at it.

Just then here comes the colonel trotting up out of the fog with Fowler. And didn't he get mad when he saw Harry and Joe rolling on the ground! He didn't say a word, but only just whipped out his pistol and bashed their heads with it until the blood ran down their faces. It made me sick to watch.

Gibson and the other three men returned soon after that with somebody new. This new man was tall and burly, and had big bulging black eyes that made him look like his head was screwed on too tight. He had on a heavy blue coat that went down to his knees and a funny hat with the front and back brims folded up and pinned together, and on his hip he wore a sword with a red tassel. There was a dog trotting along behind him—a big hound—and when he spotted the *Lady Jane* he trotted up to it and started sniffing around it. As for the man with the bulging eyes, when he saw Joe and Harry standing there with their tails between their legs he got mad and said, "What's this about, Colonel Gore?"

Colonel Gore snapped out a salute. "I'm afraid these men have been fighting, my lord," he said.

"Confound it, Colonel! If you can't control your men I'll find somebody who can. See that they're both punished after we return to the ship."

"As you wish, my lord."

"Now where's that traitor, Collins?"

"He hasn't been located yet, my lord. He may be hiding up at the lighthouse—I found a trail at the north end of the beach that leads that way. With your Lordship's permission, I'll take some of my men up there and flush him out."

"Have you looked under the boat yet?"

"The boat? Uh, no, my lord. I didn't think it necessary."

"Confound it, man! Use your head for a change. How do you know he hasn't stashed it under there? Turn her over!"

I didn't know what "it" was—probably that thing Collins said he had in his knapsack—but I was sure glad I got out from underneath the jolly boat when I did. In no time they had her flipped over. The dog went right to the spot where I'd been hiding and sniffed it; then he started off toward the woods! Here he comes, with his nose to the ground—SNIFF! SNIFF! SNIFF! I felt so sick and scared I almost passed out. He made straight for my tree, and when he was only a few feet away he stopped and brought up his head. Then he started barking! The whole beach went silent; except I could hear my heart. I thought I was a goner. But then the goggly-eyed man said, "Now what's the matter with that dog? Spartacus! Come back here, you mongrel!"

Spartacus barked one last time, for show, and then trotted back to the beach. I peeped out from behind my tree just in time to see Goggly Eyes throw out a kick that sent the poor dog yelping away with his tail between his legs. It made me so mad I wanted to run out from my hiding place and kick *him* like that, just to see how much *he* liked it. But then I figured maybe it wasn't the best time.

I saw my chance to slip away while they were distracted with the dog, so I slid out from behind the tree and tiptoed from tree to tree, making no more noise than a mouse, until the fog swallowed me up. I knew it wouldn't be long before they found their way up to the house, so I put for home as fast as I could leg it. When I got there I found Collins sitting on the floor just inside the front door, with his back against the wall and the knapsack at his feet. He looked awful glad to see me—for about half a second. Then he got mad and said, "That was a bloody stupid thing to do!"

"There's men at the cove," I blurted out. "And they have guns!"

He forgot he was mad. "Already?" he said. "Did they find the *Lady Jane*?"

I told him everything I'd seen and heard at the cove; then I showed him the pistol. His eyes fairly blazed when he saw it, and he said, "Good lad! Quick, hand me the knapsack."

I handed him the knapsack. He opened it and took out a tin box that had half a dozen little paper packets in it; they were ammunition cartridges for the pistol. He lined them up on the floor by his leg—so they'd be handy, you know—and then he gave me the knapsack and said, "Now take this and go hide in the woods. You mustn't show yourself, no matter what happens. Understand? If those men find you with that knapsack, your life won't be worth two pennies."

"But who are—"

"Shhh!" he said. "Did you hear that?"

I held my breath and listened, but all I could hear was the blare of the foghorn. Then off in the distance a dog barked. The next minute there was a yelp, and it was quiet again.

"They're coming!" he said. "Go, Orion. And remember—if they find you with that knapsack, they'll kill you!"

I didn't need any more encouragement than that; it was more than enough for me. I've never been killed before, you see, and I didn't want to find out what it felt like. So I took the knapsack and tore through the kitchen and out the back door. By that time the fog had risen over the house and the moon was making everything glow with a ghostly kind of light. I made straight for the trees in back of the house and jumped behind a big log. Then I peeped back out. I couldn't see the house now, on account of the fog being so thick, but I could make out the clump of tall grass at the place where the driveway forks. This is no good, I thought; I can't see a thing from here. I'll go hide behind that grass; then at least I can see what's going on. So I slid out from behind the log and tiptoed through the woods until I got to where the trees were nearest to the clump of grass. I stopped and listened; all still and quiet. It's now or never, I thought, and with that I jumped out of the trees and busted for the clump of grass. I was almost there, too, when all at once—BANG!—went a gun, and at the same time a man with a musket stepped out of the fog in front of me.

THE DISPATCH BOX

THAT shot saved me. It banged out just as me and the man with the musket startled one another, and what with the fog being so thick and all—well, I figured he'd shot at me, and he figured I'd shot at him. Neither of us stuck around to see if we'd get shot at again; he turned tail and bolted back into the fog, and I dove behind the clump of grass with my heart in my throat. Right after that an angry voice came booming out of the mist; it was old Goggly Eyes. "Don't be a bloody fool, Collins!" he said. "I've got an entire squad of dragoons with me. You're outnumbered and outgunned. Now throw down that pistol and come out of there!"

"Go hang!" said Collins.

I peeped over the top of the grass. There was the house, with the front door wide open, and there was Goggly Eyes, standing maybe twenty yards away, with one leg thrown out in front of him and his hands on his hips like he thought he was the Almighty Big Cheese. The colonel and his dragoons were hugging the ground around him, their guns pointed at the house. As for Collins, he was sitting on the floor where I had left him, just inside the doorway.

"Don't try my patience, Collins," said Goggly Eyes. "You have inconvenienced me no end with this tiresome business. Did you really think I'd let you escape?"

Collins didn't answer; he was busy reloading his pistol.

"Confound it, man! You're being a bloody fool. Drop that pistol and come out with my dispatch box. I'll see that you get a fair trial. Well? Don't keep me waiting."

Dispatch box—that must be what's inside the knapsack, I thought. I didn't know what a dispatch box was, or why it could be so important. But whatever it was, Collins must've swiped it from Goggly Eyes—and now he wanted it back.

"I've seen what you call a 'fair' trial," said Collins. "And I'll see you to the devil before I let you take me back!"

Goggly Eyes looked so mad I thought his head was going to explode. "Henry Collins!" he thundered. "I won't give you another chance! Are you going to return my dispatch box or not? Well, man? What do you say?"

"I say this," said Collins: "Go to the devil!"

He stuck his pistol out the door. There was a flash and a BANG!, and a cloud of black smoke filled the doorway. The next thing I knew—BANG! BANG! BANG!—muskets began to bang out all over the place.

"Hold your fire!" roared Goggly Eyes. "The next man to fire without my orders will be hanged from the yardarm, by Gad! Colonel Gore, where the devil are you? Ah, there you are. What are you doing in the dirt? Tut, tut. Get up, man."

Colonel Gore bounced up. Goggly Eyes said something to him in a low voice, then the colonel turned to Gibson and Fowler and made some signals with his hands. They jumped up with their muskets and jogged off into the fog. Whatever they were up to, I knew it couldn't be good.

I was trying to think of some way to warn Collins without giving myself away when there was a shout inside the house, and—BANG! BANG!—two shots banged out, one right after the other. Fowler and Gibson had slipped around to the back and snuck in through the kitchen door! Collins slumped over on his side and lay still. I didn't need anyone to tell me that he was dead; I just knew. I felt sick.

As the smoke cleared Gibson and Fowler appeared in the doorway. One of Gibson's arms was hooked around Fowler's shoulders; the other one hung at his side, limp and bloody.

"Well?" said Goggly Eyes.

"He's dead, my lord," said Fowler. "And Gibson's shot."

"Confound Gibson! I meant my dispatch box, you boob. Did Collins have it or not?"

"I don't rightly know, my lord."

"Confound your stupidity! Why am I always surrounded by imbeciles? Get that man back to the ship. Colonel Gore! Where the devil did you— What are you doing down there again? Get up, man, and get in that house and find my box.

Turn the place upside down if you have to, but find it, d'ye hear? Well, what are you waiting for? Go!"

The colonel and his men jumped up and ran inside, and for the next few minutes there was the wildest hullabaloo all through our old house—doors being kicked in, and furniture getting overturned, and things thrown down and smashed. At last it went quiet again, and out comes the colonel with empty hands. "It isn't there, my lord," he said.

Goggly Eyes looked fit to burst; I never saw anyone get so mad. His face went purple, and he confounded the colonel, and the colonel's men, and Collins, and the house, and the lighthouse—even the fog. Then he tried to give Spartacus a kick, but the dog saw it coming and scampered away. That just made him madder, and he began confounding everyone all over again. Meantime one of the dragoons slid up to the colonel and said something in his ear. Colonel Gore looked surprised; then he gabbed the man by the arm and marched him up to Goggly Eyes. "What is it, confound you?" he said. "Can't you see I'm busy?"

"My lord," said the colonel, "Downing here says he saw a boy with a knapsack."

I caught my breath, because now I see that Downing is the man I almost ran into in the fog. And there I was with the knapsack, close enough to hit them with a spitball. I was so scared I wanted to melt into the ground.

Goggly Eyes looked interested. "Is that so?" he said. "And just where did you see this boy, Downing?"

"In the fog, your worshipfulness," said Downing.

"Confound your insolence, man! If you don't answer me straight this time, you'll wish you were never born!"

Downing trembled so much that all they could get out of him was that he saw me somewhere between the woods and the house. He couldn't say any better than that, on account of the fog. So I breathed a little easier.

The colonel said, "The boy must be hiding in the woods, my lord. He can't be far off. With your permission, I'll take some of my men and flush him out."

"Don't be a fool, Colonel. I'll wager you a guinea that boy knows these woods like the back of his own hand. We'd be hunting for him all night. No, I have a better idea. Go back into the house and get me something that belongs to him— a hat or a shoe would answer nicely."

Colonel Gore trotted back into the house. A minute later he came back out with my baseball cap. I couldn't make out what Goggly Eyes wanted it for—until he let out a whistle, and Spartacus came running up and sniffed my cap.

Uh oh, I thought.

Spartacus put his nose to the ground and headed for the house. He disappeared inside, and then after a minute here he comes again, out the back, sniffing along the ground. He headed straight for the woods behind the house—just like I had—and the next second I lost him in the fog.

It won't be long before he finds me, I thought; I'd better think of something, and quick. But nothing came to me. If I tried to bolt they'd spot me and go for me—or just shoot me in the back, more likely—and if I stayed put Spartacus would sniff me out. I couldn't see any way out of it.

I was still trying to figure out what to do when there was a rustle behind me and Spartacus came out of the bushes. I didn't dare budge; I couldn't have anyway—I was too scared. Here he comes! Straight for my hiding place, with his nose scanning the ground and his tail going around and around like a whirligig. I was about to force myself to jump up and make a break for it when all at once he stopped and looked up at the sky. What's he doing, I wondered? Then he began to bark and jump around, the way dogs do when they know something that people don't. I couldn't make it out.

And then I heard a strange thumping noise far off in the distance, followed almost at once by a boom from the direction of the cove.

"The signal, my lord!" said the colonel.

"Confound the signal," said Goggly Eyes. "Confound the captain, too. He's afraid of his own hat."

The thumping got louder and louder by the second; then a strange glow appeared in the fog above the trees. Colonel Gore said, "My lord, we must return to the ship at once!"

"Confound that boy! I know he's got my dispatch box."

By this time the thumping was so loud I could feel the air throbbing in my ears. Goggly Eyes threw down my baseball cap and stomped on it. "Confound you, boy!" he shouted in my direction. "This isn't over yet!" Then he gave the order to return to the ship. A couple of Colonel Gore's men took Collins and they all started back to the cove, with Spartacus bounding along after them. He'd just disappeared into the fog when what looked like a gigantic orange dragonfly with blinking lights on its belly came thumping down out of the sky and landed in front of the house. It was a Coast Guard helicopter, come to take Collins to the hospital.

I jumped up and let out a whoop; the Coast Guard people were awful surprised to see me bounce up out of the grass. I told them all about Collins, and the white ship, and Goggly Eyes, and Spartacus, and the colonel and his dragoons, and how they had muskets and wore sparkly white clothes. But I didn't say anything about the dispatch box; I thought I'd let my grampa decide about that. At first they looked at me like I was a lunatic, but after they went into the house and saw that it was wrecked, and found blood on the floor and bullet holes in the walls, they began to think there might be something to it after all. So they busted out their guns and flak jackets and trooped off to the cove. But when they got there all they found was a few drops of blood leading up to the water. The *Lady Jane* was gone; so was all the wreckage. It was like she'd never even been there.

For the next couple of hours there was a real ring-dang-do at our place, with the house chock-full of people taking pictures and measurements and dusting for fingerprints and sticking little yellow flags everywhere. I couldn't turn around without bumping into somebody, with more coming every minute. My grampa came back in the middle of it all—and wasn't he mad when he saw the house! I'd never seen him in such a lather. But after he cooled down he said he'd thought all along that Collins was caught up in something shady.

The lady in charge said we'd have to stay somewhere else that night, so we packed some clothes and drove to a motel outside of town. On the way there I told my grampa about the dispatch box. He was interested, so as soon as we got to our room we looked inside the knapsack. The first thing we found was the brass spyglass that Collins used to take out to the bluff with him every day. Under that we found a parka that was stiff with sea salt and stank of fish; then came the stack of drawings, a pair of grungy mittens, a leather pouch with some strange coins in it, a pair of snow goggles, and a little wooden box that had a charcoal pencil in it. Finally, at the bottom, we found an old iron box. It was about the size of a cigar box, and on the lid there was an engraving of an eel's head between two branches.

"This must be the dispatch box," I said.

"It's locked," said my grampa. "Is there a key anywhere?"

We went through the knapsack again, but we didn't find a key. I wanted to find a hammer and smash the box open, but my grampa said it might be valuable, and we shouldn't damage it if we could help it. We put it up to our ears and shook it, but all we could hear was a soft, shuffling kind of sound, like something light was sliding across the bottom.

"Maybe we can find out about it on the computer," I said.

My grampa said it was worth a try, so we took the box to the motel office and I asked the blue-haired old lady at the counter if we could use her computer. She said we could, as long as we didn't break it. I promised her we wouldn't, and then as she peered over one shoulder and my grampa peered over the other one I typed in *dispatch box* and hit the search button. A list of links came back, along with some pictures. One of the links took us to an online encyclopedia that told us that a dispatch box was a box used to carry official papers and documents. As for the pictures, none of them looked at all like our box.

"It looks like a dead end," said my grampa.

It did look like a dead end. I was pretty disappointed.

My grampa nudged me and said it was time to let the nice lady have her computer back. I didn't want to give up, but I couldn't think of anything else to try, so I started to get up. Then I remembered the engraving.

"Wait a minute," I said. "Let me try one more thing."

I typed in *eel's head between two branches* and clicked the search button. The first link that came back took us to the website of a museum in England. The website had a picture on it of an old silver spoon, and on the handle of this spoon was an engraving of an eel's head between two branches. The description said the engraving was the crest of the Franklin family and that the spoon had once belonged to an explorer named John Franklin, who vanished in the Arctic in 1847.

"Maybe the box belonged to him," I said.

"Well," said my grampa, "if it belonged to an explorer, I know just the man to see about it."

CHAPTER 6

PROFESSOR MERIWETHER

AFTER an early breakfast the next morning we drove down to Boston and caught an express train to Washington, D.C. We pulled into the station around four o'clock, then took a cab to an old brick building in Georgetown that had a blue flag with a golden compass on it flying from the roof and a sign on the door that said "League of Explorers." There was a lady in a flowery dress sitting behind a desk in the lobby.

"Can I help you?" she said.

"We're here to see Meriwether," said my grampa.

"Is the professor expecting you today?"

"I don't know why he would be."

"Oh. Well, I suppose I can see if he's available. What name should I give him?"

"Tell him it's Patrick Poe, with his grandson."

She got up and went swishing away. About a minute later she came back and asked us to follow her. She led us down a long hallway lined with paintings of famous explorers and at the end of it showed us into an office that was filled with old books and maps, and rusty spearheads, and jade dragons and golden bowls, and little brown shrunken-down human heads dangling on necklaces and other strange things. There was a man in a rumpled suit and a bowtie standing near the window, studying a globe. He was tall and beefy, and had a cheerful kind of face that was all browned and creased by the sun. He had the grayest hair, too—except on top, where he didn't have any hair at all—and the bushiest eyebrows, and the brightest, bluest eyes I ever saw.

When he saw us he busted out in a smile, and came over and shook my grampa's hand with both of his. "Pat!" he says. "It's so good to see you. What's it been now? Ten years?"

"Hullo, Charles," said my grampa.

"And you must be Orion," he said to me, and he shook my hand, too, just the same way. "Why, you're the very spitting image of your fath— Well! How old are you now?"

"Eleven," I said.

"Eleven! I would've said twelve or thirteen. You're tall for eleven. Isn't he, Pat?"

My grampa said he supposed so.

"I bet you didn't know that your grandfather and I went to college together," said the professor. "We had some wild times, too. Why, he nearly got us expelled once. Ha, ha, ha! I'm sure he'll tell you about it when you're a little older."

"A lot older," said my grampa.

"All right, then: a lot older. Ha, ha! Anyway, what brings you down this way, Pat?"

"Orion was hoping you could tell him about an explorer named Franklin. John Franklin, I think it is."

The professor looked at me, all curious-like. "Is this for a school project?" he said.

"Something like that," I said.

"All right. Well, let's see. John Franklin was a rear admiral in the British Royal Navy, and he was also one of the most famous explorers of the nineteenth century. He was looking for the Northwest Passage in 1847 when he vanished along with his crew. The entire expedition—over a hundred and thirty men and two tall ships—disappeared without a trace. People have been looking for them ever since."

"Did he have a dispatch box with him?"

"A what?"

"A dispatch box. You know, for his papers."

"Well, yes, I suppose he did. Why?"

"Because we were wondering if this might be it."

I'd brought the knapsack with me, and I took the dispatch box out and showed it to him. He looked surprised at first; then puzzled. He examined it, and then went over to one of his bookcases and got down a book that had a picture in it of the Franklin family crest. Next he got a magnifying glass and compared the picture to the engraving on the dispatch box. They looked the same in every way; perfectly identical.

"How did you come by this?" he said.

My grampa told him he'd better sit down, and after he did I told him the story of how I came by the dispatch box—and didn't he just stare the whole time, and look from me to my grampa and back to me again! And when he heard how I ran back to the cove to get the pistol his eyes just sparkled, and he slapped his thigh and said, "Attaboy! Ha, ha, ha!"

When I finished he shook his head and said, "If that isn't the strangest story I've ever heard, I'll eat my own head. It's a puzzle, too—and I bet we'll find the answer in this box. Shall we open it?"

"We don't have the key," I said.

"Oh, we won't let a little thing like that stop us. Besides, these old boxes can usually be opened with a skeleton key. The question is, do I have the right one?"

He opened a drawer that was full of all kinds of old junk and began rummaging through it. "No," he says, "this is for a Chubb lock. How about this one? No; too small." Finally he held up a funny-looking brass key that was about twice as big as a regular house key and said, "Aha!" He worked it into the lock, and the next minute we heard a click.

"Now," he said, "let's see what we've got."

He opened the box. There was nothing inside but a piece of sealskin that had been folded into a little square and tied with a bit of string. The professor borrowed my pocketknife to cut the string, and then me and my grampa looked over his shoulders while he opened up the sealskin. There was a map of an island drawn on it. The island was shaped like a dragon's head when looked at from the side, and had a big bay at the bottom, between where the neck and jaw would be, and a mountain where the eye would be. This mountain was called Mount Erebus. There was another mountain to the south of it called Mount Terror. (I got all goosebumpy when I saw that; I wondered if that was where "the Terror" lived.) Between the mountains there was a valley called the Valley of Crevasses. A trail of X's led up to the valley from the bay, and at the end of this trail somebody had scribbled "Laughing Devil." The same person had also written "New Britain" at the top of the map, along with the latitude and longitude; and at the bottom, in the right-hand corner, we could make out a set of initials and a date: "JF, 1847."

Me and my grampa couldn't make heads or tails of it, but the professor was just beside himself. "Remarkable!" he said. "This map was drawn by Franklin himself. These X's must show where he and his men camped as they made their way across the island. And this bay down at the bottom must be where they anchored their ships. Let's see what we can find out about this island."

He took down an atlas and looked up the island from the latitude and longitude on the map. The island shown in the atlas looked exactly like the one on the map, except it had a different name and part of the interior was blank.

"Remarkable," he said. "This is one of the most secluded islands in the Canadian Arctic. Only the southern part has ever been explored, and this bit of the northeast coast here, around Cape Deception. I seem to remember there being a legend associated with this island. What was it, again? Oh, that's right. The Inuit people believe this island is inhabited by evil spirits—they call them 'bone-crushing demons,' or something like that."

He pulled a pipe out of his pocket, and lit it and began to pace back and forth, smoking and thinking. After a minute he said, "This whole business puzzles me. Who was Collins? And how did he get this map? And those men who hunted him down, who were they? I suppose there's really only one way to get to the bottom of it—I have to go."

"To the island, you mean?" I said.

"That's right. And I know Hinckley will want to come."

"Who's Hinckley?"

"Marcus Hinckley, my expedition partner. He'll jump at the chance to go with us."

"Us?" said my grampa. "What do you mean by *us*?"

"I mean us, Pat. You, me—and Orion."

I almost went over backwards; it was the last thing I ever expected. He went on and said, "Pat, you always used to say you would've been an explorer if you hadn't been drafted. Well, this is your chance. And Orion should come because if it weren't for him we wouldn't have the map. Of course, he'll have to remain aboard the *Sea Leopard*, our expedition ship. He's a bit too young to go tramping across glaciers."

"Hold on, Charles," said my grampa. "I have a lighthouse to look after, remember? Besides, the spark died out of me a long time ago. But I don't see why Orion can't go."

I couldn't believe I'd heard him right. "You mean I can go by myself?" I said.

"I don't see why not. Boys shouldn't be coddled. Did you know that when your dad was your age I drove him out to Echo Lake and left him for a week with nothing but a rifle, a box of matches, and a pocketknife? He loved it."

"So I can really go?"

"If the professor here will promise to keep you safe, yes."

Professor Meriwether laughed. "Don't you worry, Pat," he said. "I'm sure that nothing will go wrong."

I GET MY SAILING ORDERS

THE next day we went home. My grampa wasn't going to let a bunch of hoodlums with antique muskets scare him away from his own house, so he got his hunting rifle down out of the attic and leaned it against the wall near the front door. We spent the next two or three days putting the house back together—sweeping up broken glass, and fixing chairs, and patching bullet holes and whatnot—and then things pretty much went back to normal. My grampa drank his bottle of wine and fell asleep in his favorite chair every night, while I traded superhero cards and hung out with Dell and the rest of the boys. They all knew about Collins getting killed and carried away by the men in the white ship—the whole town did by then—but they didn't know about John Franklin or the map. I was just itching to tell them about it, and about the professor and how I was going on an expedition to look for a lost explorer, but my grampa didn't want me to; he said it might stir up more trouble, and we'd already had enough for one summer. Anyway we didn't see the white ship again, and after a week the rifle went back up to the attic.

The rest of July and August flew by, and September came around. I was beginning to wonder if Professor Meriwether had forgotten about me when one morning, as me and my grampa were about to eat breakfast, the mailman delivered a large box with my name on it. Inside we found enough gear to fill two duffle bags—parkas, and caps, and mittens, and long johns, and goggles, and climbing helmets, and ice axes, and boots and crampons, and everything else you'd need for an expedition to the top of the world. There was a letter in there, too, from the professor. I knew my grampa would be curious to know what it said, so I read it out loud:

> *Aboard the Sea Leopard*
> *Halifax Harbour, N.S.*
> *1 September*
>
> *Greetings, Orion!*
> *By now you must be wondering if I'd forgotten you. Well, I haven't. It's just that I had a setback while organizing the expedition, and it took a while to sort out. But everything is shipshape now, and we're ready to put to sea.*

The Sea Leopard is docked in Halifax Harbour. She's a fine ship, with a top speed of seventeen knots. She was just last year overhauled and refitted for polar service. Her captain is a dear old friend of mine by the name of Thaddeus Crump. He can be prickly at times, and he doesn't suffer fools; but he knows his business, and in a pinch there's no one better to have at your side.

"Grampa," I said, "what does it mean not to suffer fools?"

"It means you better not pull any shenanigans around the captain, or he might just throw you overboard."

I couldn't tell if he was kidding, so I made up my mind I wouldn't pull any shenanigans around Captain Crump, just to be safe. Anyway, back to the letter:

The captain is anxious to get under way. The sea north of New Britain has already frozen over, and he's afraid if we don't leave soon the ice will move farther south and keep us from reaching the island. Nobody wants that!

As for that little setback I mentioned earlier—remember Marcus Hinckley, my expedition partner? Well, the day after he agreed to join our expedition he fell

off a ladder and broke his leg. Imagine
that! Here's a young fellow who ventures
into some of the most treacherous places
on Earth and rarely gets a scratch, and
he breaks his leg falling off a ladder!
It really does make you wonder.

Anyway I had to find someone to
replace him—it would be too risky to
search for Franklin on my own. I called
every explorer I know, but no one was
available on such short notice. Then I
heard through the friend of a friend of
a friend about a young Australian who
was looking for an expedition to join.
His name is Peerless Jones, and from
what I could gather he's an experienced
jungle guide and mountaineer—though
I must say (just between the two of us)
that when I spoke to him on the phone
he seemed quite full of himself. Professor
Cratchet, a colleague of mine here at
the League of Explorers, thought he'd
heard Jones's name in connection with
a scandal in Bengkulu five years ago—
something to do with a stolen artifact
and a Chinese gangster named Lu—but
he wasn't sure it was the same fellow,
and I never got to the bottom of it.

CHAPTER 7

*I asked Jones about it, but he swore he'd
never even been to Bengkulu, and since
I had no reason to doubt him I decided
to offer him Hinckley's place.*

*Tell your grandfather I expect the
expedition to take about six weeks
altogether—two weeks to reach the
island, two weeks for Jones and me to
hike up to the Valley of Crevasses and
search for Franklin, and another two
weeks for the voyage back to Halifax.
You'll miss more school than I thought
you would, but I have a feeling you
won't mind that too much.*

*Everything you'll need is in the box.
You must be in Halifax no later than
noon on Saturday the 5th—*

"Saturday!" I said. "That's the day after tomorrow."

"Your flapjacks are getting cold," said my grampa. "Hurry
up and finish that letter." So I finished the letter:

*Ask your grandfather to call me so I'll
know where to collect you. Until then—
Over and out,
Charles Meriwether, L.O.E.
P.S. Don't be late! Captain Crump is a
stickler for promptness.*

It wasn't until I read that letter that it all really sank in: I was going on an expedition—a real one, with a real explorer leading it. I knew I had to stay aboard the *Sea Leopard* and all, but still—a real expedition!

Everything in the box fit me perfectly, and the next day, after dinner, I tossed my duffle bags and the knapsack into my grampa's truck and climbed in beside him. As we started down the driveway I looked back at the only house I'd ever really known, and at the little red-and-white lighthouse next to it. Then we dropped over the hill and they were gone.

We arrived in Bangor at quarter past ten. By the time we pulled into the bus station people were already boarding the bus, so we got my ticket and went straight to the platform. When it came my turn to board my grampa said he hoped I would listen to Professor Meriwether, and not do anything foolish or forget to have a good time, either. Then he shook my hand and walked away. I got the last seat on the bus, all the way at the back next to the window, and a few minutes later the bus rolled out of the station. We crossed the border into Canada just after midnight. I must've fallen asleep soon after that, because the next thing I can remember was being shaken by the driver, and waking to find the bus empty and the sun shining in through the windows.

I was just getting my duffle bags down when here comes Professor Meriwether, in the same rumpled suit and bowtie, wading out of the crowd with a cheery look on his face.

"There you are, Orion!" he said. "You must be as hungry as a hawk. Let's get some breakfast, shall we?"

CHAPTER 7

"All right," I said. "And after that we'll see the ship?"

"Yes," he said with a laugh. "After that we'll see the ship!"

THE *SEA LEOPARD*

WE had breakfast at a little diner across the street from the bus station, and then took a cab down to the harbor. It was crowded with ships—more than at Eastport and Bangor put together, and just about every kind and size you can imagine. There were ferries and freighters, and fishing boats, and cruise ships painted up all bright and festive; and alongside the wharf the prettiest little schooner I ever saw. It was the finest kind of day, too, with the sun sparkling off the water, and the flags snapping in the breeze, and the clouds chasing each other's shadows over the ground. But best of all the air had that sharp, salty kind of smell that makes you want to drop everything and go on an adventure. And I was!

Before I knew it we were alongside the *Sea Leopard*. The professor had been right about her—she *was* a fine ship. She was a little smaller than I had imagined, but just as trim and handsome as could be, with a fresh coat of paint and a high, graceful kind of bow. She looked like she could handle anything the sea might throw at her. I hoped so, anyway.

The first officer, Mr. McClintock, met us at the top of the gangway and welcomed us aboard. After that he took us up to the bridge and asked us to wait there while he went and got the captain. A minute or two later the door opened and in walked the captain. I didn't need anyone to tell me he was the captain, because he just looked like one. He was around sixty or so and had a stern kind of face, with a stern jaw and stern black eyes that shined out at you from underneath his bushy eyebrows. His hair was as white as chalk and cut real short; so was his beard. I only had to take one look at him to know that he wasn't someone I wanted to get on the wrong side of.

"Morning, Thaddeus," the professor said. "This is Ori—"

"That can wait, Charles," said the captain. "Have you seen the latest batch of satellite images?"

"Yes, I looked at them last night. Why?"

"No, I mean the ones that came in this morning. The ice has pushed another fifty miles south in the last twenty-four hours. The western end of Barrow Strait is almost completely blocked now. We should've put to sea two weeks ago."

"I know, and we would have if Marcus hadn't broken his leg. Anyway, it can't be helped now. We'll just have to push on and hope for the best."

"It's risky, that's all. It would be better to wait until spring."

"You're being too cautious, Thaddeus. The *Sea Leopard* is a first-rate icebreaker."

"Then I take it you're firm on going?" said the captain.

"Like steel," said the professor.

"I thought as much. In that case there are a few things we need to discuss before we put to sea. Three, to be precise."

"All right. Shoot."

"The first is that our late start makes it much more likely we'll run into sea ice—so I'd like to take a few precautions."

"Such as?"

"Such as bringing more food and fuel—at least enough so we can winter over if we get stuck in the ice. Right now we have enough supplies to last for three months. We ought to have enough for six. We should also bring more rifles."

"Why? I'm bringing one, and so is Jones."

"Yes, but there are twelve of us aboard, not counting the boy. If the ship gets stuck in the ice everyone should be able to go out onto the ice without having to worry about polar bears. That means each man should have a rifle."

"I see. Is that all?"

"Not quite. There are only two sledges aboard. Why not bring one for every man? That way we could get all our gear and provisions across the ice if we had to abandon ship."

"Abandon ship! Really, Thaddeus, it could never come to that. The *Sea Leopard* is unsinkable."

The captain gave a little jump. "You must never say that, Charles!" he said. "That's what they said about the *Titanic*, and look what happened to her. Now take it back."

"Okay. But I still don't see how it could come to that."

"I agree that it's unlikely, but we lose nothing by taking a few extra sledges along. I'd much rather have them and not need them than the other way around."

"I hear you. Is that everything?"

"As far as the extra precautions are concerned, yes. I took the liberty of ordering everything in advance, and it can all be brought aboard and stowed before the evening tide. You just have to give the okay. And pay the bill, of course."

The professor didn't look happy, and he mumbled something about the expedition already being over budget; but in the end he gave his approval. After that he asked the captain what the second thing was.

"Ah, yes," said the captain. "It has to do with that fellow you found to stand in for Hinckley."

"Peerless Jones? What about him?"

"Do you remember Pierce Flanagan, captain of the *Petrel* out of Kuala Lumpur?"

"Vaguely. Was he that fellow with the glass eye?"

"No, that was Dawkins. Flanagan was the other fellow, the one who socked that boneheaded pilot on the nose after he ran us aground. Anyway, McClintock bumped into him at the Brass Monkey last night, and they fell to talking."

"About Jones?"

"That's right. I don't know how his name came up, but it hardly matters. Anyway, it seems that two or three years ago an archeologist named Chowser hired Flanagan to transport his expedition up the Mekong river. After dinner one night

Chowser happened to mention that he'd once hired a jungle guide called Peerless Jones to escort himself and a colleague into the Kingdom of Bhutan to look for a lost temple. They found it, but only after weeks of hardship and the death of the colleague, who apparently was killed by a tiger. Anyway, an early monsoon forced them to leave the area before they could excavate the temple. The following year Chowser went back to the site—without Jones—and, guess what?"

"The temple had been looted?" said the professor.

"That's right. Now as far as Chowser knew, Jones was the only other person in the world who knew the location of that temple. So if I were you I'd keep an eye on him."

"Duly noted. And the third thing?"

The captain gave me a stern look. "It's about the boy," he said. "Since you ignored my advice and brought him along anyway, we'll have to make the best of it. The *Sea Leopard* is a working ship, and I don't want him getting underfoot."

"What do you have in mind?"

"Mess boy. Baldy could use him in the galley."

"How does that sound to you, Orion?"

I said it sounded all right, even though I didn't know what a mess boy was; but you can be sure I didn't like the captain after that. He picked up the intercom and ordered someone named Baldy to report to the bridge. Half a minute later a man stuck his head in. "You wanted me, sir?" he said.

"Come in, Baldy," said the captain. "This is the boy I was telling you about. Make sure he stays out of the men's way. You can put him up in Ben Johnson's old bunk."

"Yes, sir," said Baldy.

He stared at me, and I at him. He looked about the same age as the captain, and had a friendly face and gold rings in his ears. I couldn't see why they called him Baldy, because he had more hair than most people; it was long and gray and pulled back into a ponytail. He wore a grubby white apron that was covered with grease. He wiped his hands on it and said, "Does the boy have a name, sir?"

"Does the boy have a name, Charles?" said the captain.

For once I got in ahead of the professor.

"It's Orion, Mr. Baldy," I said.

"Just Baldy, son," he said with a laugh. "Baldy Brownlow, at your service. Why don't you come with me, and I'll show you the ship. Here, let me take one of them duffles."

He took one of my duffle bags and I followed him below. He showed me my bunk, which used to belong to someone named Ben Johnson who I later found out died, and then he took me around the ship and introduced me to the crew and showed me where everything was. After that he took me to the galley and showed me my duties. He kept me busy for the rest of that morning and afternoon, setting the table for lunch, and washing up the dishes afterward, and taking the scraps bucket up to the deck and emptying it over the side, and sharpening knives, and scrubbing pans, and whatever else he wanted me to do. By the time I finished my chores and went up to the deck to see what was happening it was nearly dark. The extra fuel and provisions had been brought aboard and stowed away by then, and the crew were leaning on the rail, smoking and looking out over the water. Captain Crump was pacing on the bridge deck, stopping every now and then to check his watch. He looked mighty sour. As for the professor, he was standing by the gangway, talking with Mr. McClintock. He looked sour, too. They both did.

It didn't take long to find out why. Peerless Jones hadn't showed up yet, and the captain was worried that if we didn't cast off soon we'd miss the evening tide.

Another hour dragged by, and it was starting to look like we were going to miss our tide altogether when a cab pulled alongside the *Sea Leopard*. A man got out and came rolling up the gangway like he had all the time in the world. He looked around thirty or so, and had quick little eyes and a face with a sneaky kind of look to it; you could almost call it a "crocodilish" look. His getup was pretty crocodilish, too. He had one of those funny hats they like to wear down there in Australia—you know, the kind with the flat top and the crocodile teeth in the band—and a crocodile skin vest, and crocodile boots; and what had to be the biggest rifle I'd ever seen. To top it off he was smoking a big fat cigar, and as he came sauntering up the gangway he worked his jaw so that it swapped from one side of his mouth to the other.

"Where have you been, Jones?" said the professor. "We've almost missed our tide!"

"G'day to you, too," said Peerless. "I reckon you must be Meriwether. What was that about the tide?"

"Oh, never mind. But in the future I expect you to be on time. Are we clear on that?"

"Whatever you say, mate. You don't need to throw a wobbly over it." Then he jerked his head at Mr. McClintock and said, "Who's this bloke?"

"This gentleman is our first officer, Mr. McClintock."

"Uh-huh." Next he jerked his head at *me*. "And is this the little ankle biter that got us the map?"

"This is the young man who brought us the map, yes. His name is Orion Poe."

"I don't care if it's Harry Potter, mate, just so long as you don't ask me to babysit him. I didn't sign up for that."

He ground his cigar out under his heel and wandered off to his cabin. Mr. McClintock clapped his hands behind his back and stared after him, looking as dark as a thundercloud. The professor didn't look too happy, either.

As for me, if I'd been bigger I would have picked him up and chucked him over the side—hat, rifle, and all.

THE VOYAGE NORTH

AS soon as Peerless's gear was brought aboard and stowed the captain gave the order to put to sea. Mr. McClintock passed the order along, and all of a sudden the engines were rumbling to life, and the crew were flicking their cigarettes over the side and jumping to the lines, and the gangway was being reeled in. Then the horn let out a blast and the wharf began to fall away; soon the breakwater was behind us, and just like that I was on my way to the top of the world.

As things turned out it took longer to get there than the professor thought it would—and we almost didn't get there at all, as you'll see. But Professor Meriwether was right about one thing: the captain knew his business.

Captain Crump was a sea captain through and through. You could say he was born to it—his dad was a sea captain,

and so was *his* dad, and so was *his* dad, too, going all the way
back to the days of the clipper ships. Every day he'd wear a
crisp white captain's hat and a black sweater with three gold
bars on each shoulder; except on Sundays he would put on
a black coat that had two rows of shiny brass buttons down
the front, and then he'd bring out an old dog-eared Bible his
dad gave him and hold services on the foredeck, and you had
to come. He didn't put up with any shenanigans—he hated
shenanigans—and if he ever told you to do something you'd
better jump to it. I never heard him laugh or saw him smile.
Baldy told me he saw him smile once, about thirty years ago.
Captain Crump expected the *Sea Leopard* to be shipshape at
all times, and if he ever saw anything he didn't like his face
would cloud over and his eyes start to smolder; and then you
wanted to slink away and hide somewhere until it blew over.
But he never raised his voice, except when he wanted to be
heard above the wind—and then he could roar.

Every night he'd invite the professor and Peerless to have
dinner with him and the other two officers in his cabin. After
dinner he'd go over to a special cabinet that only he had the
key to and break out a box of cigars and a bottle of brandy,
and they'd all sit around the table and drink and smoke and
talk; except the captain would just smoke and talk. Peerless
mainly talked. And talked, and talked; you couldn't shut him
up. He had opinions about everything, and he wasn't at all
shy about telling you what they were. Mr. McClintock had
his opinions, too, and since they were always the opposite of
Peerless's it wasn't long before they hated each other.

Mr. McClintock was forty, and had a lean and handsome face that reminded me of a hawk. I couldn't call him by his first name, Leo; I had to call him *Mister* McClintock. Only Captain Crump and the professor could call him by his first name, and they only ever did it when none of the crew were around. The other officer was Mr. Clark, the engineer. His head was as smooth and shiny as a bowling ball. He kept an old rag in his back pocket, and whenever he got upset about anything he'd pull it out and polish his head with it. He was nice enough, but he could be a little gruff sometimes.

As for the crew, they called themselves the Sea Leopards after the ship. Baldy was one of the oldest; he'd been sailing with Captain Crump for over thirty years. Only one other Sea Leopard had been with the captain longer, and that was Bill Turner. Bill was the crustiest, saltiest character you ever met; a real "sea dog," as my grampa would say. He was about seventy, but he looked more like a hundred and ten. Baldy said hard living was what did it.

There used to be another Sea Leopard by the name of Ben Johnson, who fell overboard in a storm and drowned before they could fish him out. Baldy told me about it. He said he saw a shark following the ship before the storm, so he knew *somebody* was going to die. He just didn't know who.

On the third day out of Halifax a seabird began following the ship. He would glide along in our wake all morning and afternoon, like a kite on a string; then in the evening when I emptied the bucket of food scraps over the side he'd swoop down and pick out what he wanted. It was really something to see him gliding along back there, day after day, without once stopping to rest. Baldy said it was a good sign. "You'll see, Orion," he said to me one day. "Nothing'll go wrong as long as he's watching over us." He was right, too; nothing did go wrong. We had the best weather, with calm seas and not a wisp of fog, and no one fell overboard. Before long the Sea Leopards began calling the bird "Ben Johnson," because seabirds are supposed to carry the souls of drowned sailors and they thought he carried Ben's. The professor said it was nonsense. "But don't ever tell them that," he said to me one evening when we were alone. "Sailors take these things very seriously. Even the captain."

Meanwhile things between Mr. McClintock and Peerless went from bad to worse. Most of the trouble happened on account of Peerless's rifle. He loved that rifle, and every day he would sit on the aft deck, polishing it and talking to it. That was all right, I suppose. But then whenever one of the Sea Leopards happened by Peerless would call him over and chew his ear off about how powerful his rifle was, and what a great shot he was with it, and so on and so forth until you wanted to barf. Then Mr. McClintock would come striding along and see what was going on. He would clap his hands behind his back and say, pretty short and sharp, "This man has work to do, Jones. I thought I asked you not to speak to the men while they're on duty." Then off he'd go. Peerless would look as mad as a snake and mutter, "Bloody piker! I wish he'd pull his lip over his head and swallow."

It would've been okay if that was all the trouble that came

from that rifle, but it wasn't. One evening, about ten days out of Halifax, I was dumping the scraps over the side when Peerless spotted me and said, "Hey, Orion! Come over here for a second." So I went over to see what he wanted. "Take a look at this baby," he said, holding up his rifle. "Ain't she a beauty? Stainless steel barrel, all-weather finish, hardened cross bolts—wait, where are you going? You ain't seen the best part yet. Look at this: a round feed with a non-rotating claw extractor! What d'ya think of that?"

I'd seen it a million times before, so I said, "I think I hear Baldy calling me," and started to go. He grabbed my sleeve and reeled me back in.

"Baldy, schmaldy," he says. "He can wait. Did you know this baby can send a bullet a half a mile in one second? But she's got a wicked kick—don't you, baby?"

"I better go before Mr. McClintock comes along," I said.

He got mad. "McClintock can go dance with the dingoes for all I care," he said. "Speaking of dingoes, did I tell you I once nailed a dingo from six hundred yards with this baby?"

I couldn't believe anybody could hit something that small from so far away, and I said as much. But I wished I hadn't, because then he says, "You don't believe me? Watch this."

He jumped up, and flicked off the safety and aimed at the sky. CRACK! went the rifle—and Ben Johnson exploded in a cloud of feathers. I almost swallowed my tongue.

The shot brought everyone running aft. The Sea Leopards were outraged when they found out what Peerless had done; Mr. McClintock would have thrown him over the side right then and there if the professor hadn't stopped him. Peerless couldn't understand what the fuss was about; he said it was only a stupid bird, and sulked off to his cabin.

The Sea Leopards took it pretty hard. Later that night, in the galley, Baldy said, "I'll tell you something, Orion. There ain't nothing worse than killing a seabird. Ben's soul was in there, and now it's going to want revenge, as sure as eggs is eggs. Mark my words—our luck's about to change."

His words were still ringing in my head when Bill Turner shoved his head into the galley and sang out, "Iceberg!"

CHAPTER 10

OUR BATTLE AGAINST THE ICE

WE ran up to the deck. There was a band of haze along the horizon, and in it we could make out a monster slab of ice that was a mile long and as tall as a building. The wind and currents pushed it across our bow, and not long after that it disappeared over the horizon. Then here comes a whole fleet of them sailing along, looking all stately and solemn, like a parade of warships. Baldy said it was a bad omen.

When I came up on deck the next morning the sea ahead was covered with ice. It looked like a gigantic white jigsaw puzzle. Some of the pieces were pushed together, and others floated apart, with lanes of water between them. Most of the lanes were closed off, like ponds, but some stretched on for miles, like rivers. I could see them opening and closing as the wind and currents pushed the floes around.

We eased into a lane that ran north and followed it to the end, about nine miles. There was another lane just ahead on the other side of a floe, but I didn't see how we were going to get to it; we seemed to be stuck. But Captain Crump just backed the ship up, then told everybody to brace themselves and drove full speed at the floe. The bow rode up and over it, and the weight of the ship came crashing down and split the floe in half. Then we shouldered the pieces aside and pulled into the other lane. Sometimes the floes would get all backed up like a traffic jam, and we'd have to wait as much as a day before they loosened up and started moving again. We also had to keep an eye out for icebergs—the wind would push them through the pack like enormous snowplows. We could hear them thundering off in the distance, and even though they were miles away it still made us jittery.

It went like that for three weeks. Then one day I woke up around dawn and was having a stretch when I noticed how quiet it was—no engines rumbling, no water gurgling along the hull; total silence. So I rolled out of bed, all curious, and went up to the deck. As far as I could see in every direction the sea looked like it had been whipped up by a giant hand and then suddenly frozen in place; there were blocks of ice as big as churches piled on top of one another and floes shoved up into ridges thirty feet high. A few miles to the southeast there was a big iceberg thundering through the pack.

I found Professor Meriwether at the bow; he was smoking his pipe and staring at a dark smudge on the horizon. When I squinted I could make out two humps in the middle of it.

"What *is* that?" I said.

"That's New Britain," he said. "We're only about twenty miles away, but we won't be able to get any closer until this ice breaks up. And by the looks of it, that could be a while."

Later that morning Captain Crump let us go down onto the ice to stretch our legs. Somebody brought a soccer ball, and we made goalposts out of snow and played a game while Mr. McClintock stood on the deck with a rifle and kept an eye out for polar bears. We couldn't have ordered up better weather, with the sky as clear as crystal and not a breath of wind, and everywhere the snow so white it hurt our eyes to look at it. In the afternoon Professor Meriwether shot a seal, and that evening Baldy cooked it and we had seal steaks for dinner. I'd never had seal before. It was awful greasy; but if I slathered enough ketchup on it I didn't notice as much.

Next day was the same; just the nicest weather, and not a puff of wind. But on the third day a breeze sprang up from the south. That was good; we wanted the wind to blow so it would loosen the pack and open up some lanes. Well, toward evening some lanes did open up, and one of them snaked all the way to the island. But there was a good thirty yards of ice between the *Sea Leopard* and the lane. The professor was anxious to reach the island, and so he wanted to clear a path through the ice with picks and shovels. But the captain said it would be easier to move Mount Everest. He thought that the pack would break up in another day or two anyway, so it would be best to wait. It seemed to me he was right. That ice was a good five feet thick, and I didn't see how we could cut a path through it by hand. A few truckloads of dynamite could've done it, maybe.

We went to bed that night hoping the pack would break up the next day like the captain thought it would. Then just after midnight we were woken by a noise that sounded like a nuclear bomb going off. A second later we heard a strange rumbling coming toward us, and then a tremendous shudder went through the ship. I grabbed my parka and hurried up to the deck along with everybody else. The sky was as black as ink, and just brimming over with stars, except off to the south there was a patch of sky on the horizon where there *weren't* any stars; just solid blackness. It grew as we watched it. At first I couldn't figure out what it was. And then it hit me—it's an iceberg, and it's heading straight for the ship!

The captain started throwing out orders, and in no time the deck lights were all a-blaze, and the gangway was being lowered down to the ice, and everyone was grabbing a pick, or a shovel, or whatever else they could get their hands on and hurrying down the gangway to cut a path through the ice so the *Sea Leopard* could get to the lane. I grabbed a pick and went out with them; I wasn't going to sit around while some iceberg tried to run me over.

Our only hope was to clear a path to the lane before the iceberg rolled over us, so we went right to work. But the ice was as hard as concrete, and we couldn't seem to do much more than chip away at it. To make everything worse, as the night went on it got colder and colder, until the loose snow that was sitting on top of the pack froze into tiny little ice crystals, like dust. The wind whipped it up, and before long there was so much snow dust clogging the air that we could hardly see a thing. And all along the iceberg was thundering in our ears, and swallowing more and more of the sky.

Two hours into this miserableness Captain Crump called a break; we'd hardly made a dent in the ice, and we were all exhausted. He'd just ordered Baldy to run aboard and make some coffee when there was a noise like a thunderclap, and the pack lurched so hard I got thrown off my feet.

The captain helped me up. "Run on up to the crow's nest and tell me what you see," he said.

So I ran back aboard and climbed up to the crow's nest. I was above all the snow dust now, so I *could* see. And what I saw was a wall of ice that towered over us like a tsunami.

"There's a new ridge!" I hollered down.

"How far away?" the captain hollered back.

"About a hundred yards!"

"All right—come down!"

By the time I got down the captain had called everybody together. "There's no point in continuing," he said, looking grim. "We'll never make it to the lane before that ridge hits the ship. You'll have to take your chances on the ice."

"What do you mean, *you?*" said Professor Meriwether.

"I'm staying with the ship," the captain said.

"Like heck you are!"

"I'm not going to argue with you, Charles. You know the captain always stays with his ship." And he looked so fierce and determined that the professor didn't argue back.

I never saw such chaos and confusion as there was during the next hour, with everyone tearing this way and that and running into everyone else in the rush to get all of our gear off the *Sea Leopard* before the ridge struck her. We'd only carried half of it down to the ice when the foot of the ridge reached the ship and began to roll her over. Captain Crump ordered the crew to run ropes across the decks so we could cross them; when they became too steep to use the ropes he had the crew put up ladders. By the time we got the last of our gear off the ship she was almost on her side.

We threw everything onto our sledges, and then everyone except me put on a harness and hitched himself to a sledge. I wanted to pull one, too, but the professor said they were too heavy, and he didn't want me to slow us down.

When we were ready to go the captain climbed down off the ship and came over. "I've notified the authorities of our situation," he said. "There's an abandoned weather station on the northeast side of the island, at Cape Deception. You can take shelter there until a ship can be sent for you. I have no doubt that Professor Meriwether will get you there safely. There's no better man for the job."

He shook hands with each of us and marched back to the ship. We watched him go, and then we turned our backs on the doomed *Sea Leopard* and set off across the frozen sea.

ACROSS THE FROZEN SEA

THERE were twelve of us altogether, and we trooped along in single file, with Professor Meriwether out in front and Mr. McClintock bringing up the rear. As soon as we got clear of the *Sea Leopard's* lights it was so dark we had to turn on our headlamps, and even then all I could see was the professor's tracks running ahead into the darkness. The ice groaned and complained all around us, and every now and again a noise that sounded like a cannon going off would come booming out of the darkness, and we knew an ice floe had split in half close by. It gave me the creepiest feeling—like I was making my way through an old house that was full of restless ghosts.

Around four o'clock the wind fell off, and soon after that the moon came up, all bright and silvery, and made it almost as light as day. Up ahead on the horizon we could make out a dark outline that looked like a mountain range. It cheered me up considerably, because I thought it was the island. But when we got closer I saw that it wasn't the island at all, but what they call a "pressure ridge," which is a ridge that's made when one ice floe rides up over another one. It was fifty feet high and had a steep, craggy face with deep cracks running through it. I climbed to the top with Professor Meriwether and Peerless and Mr. McClintock and looked out. Just more ice was all we could see, stretching away to a black line on the horizon. *That* was the island.

Professor Meriwether thought it would take too long to go around the ridge, so we got out some ropes and hauled the sledges over it. They were awful heavy, and to make it even harder they kept sliding sideways and getting wedged in the cracks. It took us more than an hour to get them all over.

By the time we were ready to start off again the sky was beginning to gray up in the east; then almost before I knew it the moon had sunk down out of sight on one side of the world and the sun had come up on the other, all grand and glorious—and it was daytime.

We hiked all morning without a break and made between ten and twelve miles. We had a few easy stretches along the way, but mostly we were hauling the sledges across pressure ridges, and stepping through rotten ice, and getting bogged down in slush. And all the while the island was sitting there on the horizon, never looking any closer, it seemed to me. It was pretty rough going. But the professor wouldn't ease up; he seemed to be in a hurry for some reason. As the morning went on I got more and more tired. At last I couldn't keep my eyes open any longer; and then I nodded off, and slept and walked at the same time.

"Orion!" somebody said. "Wake up!"

I opened my eyes. The sky had clouded over and turned gray, and a chilly wind was blowing down from the north. The professor was standing in front of me with his hand on my shoulder—and he didn't even *look* tired.

"We're stopping here for a break," he said. "Baldy's going to fix us something to eat, and then we need to push on. Get some rest, okay? Baldy can manage without you this once."

He tramped off to tell the others, who were straggling up behind me. I found a spot behind a snowdrift where I'd be out of the wind and lay down for a nap. I'd just dropped off to sleep when the sound of voices woke me; it was Professor Meriwether and Mr. McClintock. They were on the other side of the snowdrift, and the wind was blowing their voices right to me. I heard Mr. McClintock say, "But the men are exhausted. They need to rest."

"I know," said the professor, "but we must get off the ice. The barometer's been falling fast since dawn. I think there's a blizzard on the way—and it could be a whopper."

"You mean bad enough to break up the pack?"

"That's what worries me. And of course if we don't reach the island first, we'll be dumped into the sea."

Dumped into the sea! It never crossed my mind that the ice might break up under us before we got to the island. All of a sudden I wasn't sleepy any more.

"How much time do we have?" said Mr. McClintock.

"It's hard to say. Five hours, maybe six if we're lucky."

"Five hours! But we still have nearly ten miles to go!"

"Not so loud, Leo. We don't want the men to panic. Let's just get off the ice as fast as we can."

I was all for that. So when they left I got up and went over to see how Baldy was coming along with lunch; I wanted to hurry him up if I could. But by that time lunch was almost ready. Beef and potato hotpot, rice pudding with cinnamon, and hot cocoa is what he had for us—and was it ever good! So good I almost forgot it might be the last meal I ever ate.

As soon as lunch was over the professor got everyone into their harnesses and we started off again. We hadn't gone far when here come the first snowflakes whirling down out of the sky; so he'd been right about the blizzard. Pretty soon it was snowing so hard I couldn't see the professor any longer. He didn't want anybody to get lost, so he called a halt and roped us all together.

We struggled over mostly broken pack for the next three or four hours, then along toward evening we slid down off a ridge and onto a flat stretch of ice where the going was easy. By that time the wind was just booming along, right in our faces, and the snow coming down like nobody's business. It was falling so fast I couldn't see jack; just a solid curtain of snow. The professor kept up a blistering pace anyway, never stopping but once, and then only just long enough to let us catch our breaths and have a few sips of water. That was all right—we didn't *want* to stop. We were still a mile from the island when cracks began opening up in the ice and pressure ridges started to break apart and thunder down into the sea. If that wasn't bad enough, the ice kept getting thinner and thinner, until at last it was so thin we could see killer whales cruising around underneath us. We could hear them blowing all around us, too; and sometimes they'd poke their snouts out of the cracks and eyeball us.

So we hauled for the island as fast as we could go; and the wind blew harder and harder, and the pack thundered and quaked, and the snow lashed our faces. Finally there were so many cracks opening up around us that I thought I'd better send up a prayer. I was about to do it, too, when all at once the wind fell off. Then somebody sang out: "Land ho!"

I stared into the blizzard and made out a line of high cliffs that were blocking the wind. At the foot of them there was a narrow beach littered with giant slabs of ice. And then I saw something that made my mouth go dry—there was a strip of water between the ice and the beach. It was only fifty or so yards wide, but it might as well have been fifty miles.

I thought we were all done for, but Professor Meriwether wasn't beat yet; he said we'd find a way off the ice if *he* had anything to say about it. He led us up to the edge, and then we scouted along it in both directions for as much as half a mile. We didn't see any way to get to the beach.

"There must be a way," the professor said as he stared at the beach. And then his face lit up. "Of course! Why didn't I think of it before? We'll make a raft."

"Are you bonkers?" said Peerless. "Out of what?"

"Ice. We've got plenty of it, after all."

Peerless said he must be kidding. But he wasn't, and since nobody had a better idea we set about making the raft. First we marked out a square about twenty yards across, one side being along the water, and then we moved all the sledges to the middle and began cutting out the raft with our ice axes. Everybody pitched in—even Peerless, who usually vanished whenever there was any work to be done.

When the raft was cut out we jumped aboard and pushed it out of its dock. We drifted away from the pack, and then a big swell came along and started to carry the raft toward the beach. As the swell picked up speed it began to lift the raft. "Everyone to the middle!" shouted the professor—and as everybody jumped to the middle of the raft the front and back edges broke off and went tumbling away in the surf.

Up, up, up we went, higher and higher, while the beach raced toward us. Suddenly the raft dropped out from under me, and the world turned upside down. I tumbled over and over; a roaring noise filled my ears, and glimpses of ice and gear and bodies flashed in front of my eyes.

And then just as suddenly everything went quiet again—and there I was, flat on my back, looking up at the sky.

MAROONED

LUCKILY nobody got killed, but there were plenty of scrapes and bruises to go around. Simon Killigrew, one of the Sea Leopards, got the worst of it; he bit his tongue half off *and* threw out his shoulder. The professor stuffed his mouth full of cotton, then took hold of his shoulder and said, "Ready? On three." Simon turned as white as a bean. "One," said the professor—and then POP! went the shoulder back into place. He never said the "two" or "three" at all!

As for me, all I got was a busted lip and some skin torn off my palm. The professor slapped a bandage on my hand and gave my hair a tousle.

By time all the sledges had been dragged up the beach where the sea couldn't get at them, except for one that got lost in the surf when the raft broke up. Later we found out it had our snowshoes on it, along with all of our ammunition except for a single box of rifle cartridges the professor had in his backpack. It also had two hundred pounds of dried peas on it. Nobody minded about the peas, but the ammunition was another thing, because once we'd used up that one box we'd have no way to hunt or keep the polar bears off.

We were soaked to the skin, and cold, and hungry, and so tired that all we wanted to do was bust out our sleeping bags and crash right there on the beach. But we couldn't. It was so narrow that at high tide the water came all the way up to the cliffs, and if we didn't get off it the tide would come up and wash us out to sea. So the professor sent Peerless off in one direction to look for a way up the cliffs, while him and I headed off in the other. We hiked a good two miles along the foot of the cliffs, but we didn't find a single break; just a solid wall of rock rising up into the mist. At last we came to a rocky headland that jutted out into the sea like a gigantic claw. To get around it we'd need a hot air balloon, and since neither of us had thought to bring one we had to turn back.

That's when I noticed the cave. It was tucked in behind a clump of boulders near the foot of the cliffs, and if I hadn't happened to look right at it I never would've seen it.

Now there's almost nothing I like better than a good cave, and even though I was tired I wanted to explore it, and find out how far in it went and see what might be inside it. But when I asked the professor he said no; he was worried about the tide, he said, and he wanted to get back and find out if Peerless had found a way off the beach. So we headed back.

By the time we got back to Mr. McClintock and the rest of them it was getting dark. A few minutes later here comes Peerless strolling up the beach, looking pleased and satisfied with himself. He hadn't found a way off the beach, he said, but he had found a place above the tide line where we could camp for the night. So we got the sledges and followed him down the beach. After a while we came to a narrow break in the cliffs. It wasn't very deep, and the floor sloped up pretty steeply and was covered with slippery rocks; but it was above the tide line, and at the back there was a kind of hollow in the cliffs that would give us some shelter from falling rocks. The professor gave the order to make camp.

I was pretty tired, so I crawled into my sleeping bag and figured I'd sleep until supper was ready. But I must've slept a good deal longer than that, because when I woke up again the clouds were gone and the moon was shining bright, and everyone else was sound asleep. I lay there a while, looking up at the moon and thinking about all that had happened; then I rolled over and tried to go back to sleep. But I found I couldn't. I had gotten to thinking about that cave I'd seen earlier, and wondering what was in it. I knew I wouldn't be able to rest until I went and gave it a good going-over, so I crawled out of my sleeping bag, as quiet as a cat, and put on my headlamp and slipped out of camp.

The headland was three miles from the camp, and by the time I got there the moon had dropped behind it. It was as dark as the inside of a pocket among the boulders, and even with my light I couldn't find the cave; everything looked so different in the dark. I was beginning to worry that I might get caught by the tide when I noticed a patch of darkness a shade darker than everything around it. I took a closer look, and sure enough, it was the cave.

I ducked inside. The walls were cold and clammy. When I got about thirty yards in the cave opened out into a room about the size of a large bedroom. There were three passages leading away from this room. Two of them dead-ended, but the third one led to an even bigger room. There didn't seem to be anything in it except more passages, and I didn't dare go any farther; I might not be able to find my way back. So I turned around and was just going out when something on the other side of the cave caught my eye. I shined my light on it—and what do I see sitting there with his back against the wall but a man! Well, the skeleton of a man, anyway. It scared the bejeezus out of me, being so unexpected and all, and it took all the courage I had to keep from turning tail and blazing out of there. But my curiosity was too strong; so I took a breath, and started creeping toward him.

When I got over to him I saw there wasn't anything to be scared about; *he* wasn't in any shape to be bothering anyone. He was sitting on the ground, with his back to the wall and his chin resting on his chest. There was a tattered knapsack at his side, and in it I found an old rigging knife, and some fishhooks, and a whale's tooth with a carving of a ship on it, and a clay pipe with a busted stem and some other junk like that. I knew the professor would be thrilled when I told him about it; this kind of thing was right up his alley.

I was about to go through his pockets when I felt a draft from one of the passages. That's curious, I thought. I'll just see where that passage goes; I can always follow the draft to find my way back. A few yards in the ground started to turn up. The slope got steeper and steeper, until I found myself climbing up a kind of natural shaft. Before long I noticed a dusting of snow on the rocks around me; a minute later my head popped out into the open.

I was at the top of the cliffs!

It was too dark to see much of anything, so I went down and headed back to the camp, all on fire to tell the professor about my discoveries in the morning. By the time I got there the tide was starting to lick at the foot of the cliffs, so I was glad I'd started back when I did. I crawled into my sleeping bag just as the sky was beginning to gray up in the east. My hands were raw and blistered, and I was done in.

When I woke up it was late morning, and the fog was so thick I couldn't see the beach. I wanted to tell the professor about the cave, but Baldy told me he went off with Peerless three hours earlier to look for a way up the cliffs.

About an hour later they came back, looking pretty glum. Mr. McClintock asked them if they'd had any luck.

"The cliffs are unbroken all the way down," the professor said. "It looks like we'll have to climb."

"Climb! But these cliffs must be three hundred feet high. And the men have no climbing experience."

"I'm aware of that, Leo, but unless anybody knows of an easier way up we're just going to have to climb."

"I know an easier way up," I said.

Peerless laughed. "Right," he said. "Now why don't you go make a sand castle or something, and let the grown-ups figure this out."

"Be quiet, Jones," said the professor. "Go on, Orion. Tell me about it."

So I told him how I slipped out of camp during the night and went back to the cave and explored it, and how I found the skeleton and the shaft to the top of the cliffs. I thought he'd slap me on the back and tell me how glad he was he'd brought me along, but he only looked so disappointed in me for leaving camp without telling anyone that I made up my mind I wouldn't sneak off again, if I could help it.

The tide was already beginning to come back in by then, so we threw our gear onto the sledges and dragged them up the beach to the cave. When the professor saw the skeleton he forgot he was disappointed in me, and he slapped me on the back and said he was glad he'd brought me along. Then he bent down and studied the dead man. After a minute he said, "Ho! What's this?" and pulled something shiny out of one of the man's pockets. It was a silver spoon, and on the handle there was an engraving of an eel's head between two branches. Professor Meriwether said it proved that the man had belonged to Franklin's expedition. I said maybe the man *was* Franklin, but the professor didn't think so. Franklin was a rear admiral, he said, while the dead man was dressed like a common sailor. Well, that made me wonder what he was doing with one of Franklin's silver spoons in his pocket.

Bill Turner made a cross out of driftwood and laid it on the dead man's chest, and then we all pulled off our caps—except for Peerless—and had a moment of silence. I hoped the poor man was resting easier, wherever he was, and that he hadn't gotten into too much trouble over the spoon.

By the time we got ourselves and the sledges to the top of the cliffs the fog had burned off and we could see for miles in every direction. Off to the north there was a rocky valley that ended in a glistening snowfield, and to the south the sea stretched away to the horizon. There wasn't a single piece of ice on it—and no sign of the *Sea Leopard*, either.

CHAPTER 13

MOUNT TERROR

WE made camp in a rocky hollow about a mile inland, and then hiked back out to the bluff and held a service for the captain. Peerless tried to get out of it by slinking away and hiding behind a rock when he thought the professor wasn't looking; but the professor *was* looking, and made him come. No one had a Bible, so Professor Meriwether just said a few words, and then pulled off his cap and bowed his head. Me and the Sea Leopards did the same, and nobody said a word for about a minute. Peerless just stood there the whole time, chomping on his cigar and looking bored.

By the time we got back to camp the sun had gone down. There was no wood or brush to make a fire with, so we lit a propane lantern and sat around it while we ate our supper. At first everybody was quiet; no one seemed to want to talk.

Then Baldy cleared his throat and said, "So what's the plan, Perfesser? We startin' out for Cape Deception tomorrow?"

The professor was about to answer him when Peerless said, "The plan is to hike up to the Valley of Crevasses and search for this Franklin bloke and his mates, and anything of value they might've left laying around. Ain't that why we came to this godforsaken rock?"

"Maybe you didn't notice, Jones," said Mr. McClintock, "but Captain Crump is dead and we're marooned at the top of the world. This isn't about Franklin any longer. We have to get to Cape Deception before winter sets in."

"And who are you to say what we do?" Peerless shot back. "You weren't in charge the last time I checked."

"Please, gentlemen," said the professor, "this isn't helpful. I've been studying the map, and what I was about to say is I think there's a way we can look for Franklin *and* reach Cape Deception before winter sets in. Take a look at this."

He got out the map, and everybody gathered around him while he traced out a route up to Cape Deception that would take us within a day's hike of the Valley of Crevasses. "Jones and I can branch off here," he said, "west of Mount Terror, and then make our way down to the valley while the rest of you continue toward the cape. We'll spend two or three days searching for Franklin, and then head north and rejoin you here, where these ridgelines meet. You might have to wait a day or two for us to catch up, but not more than that. And if we have any luck, by the time we reach the cape we'll find a ship waiting there to take us home."

Peerless and Mr. McClintock were satisfied with the plan, but Baldy just shrugged. "I suppose it don't really matter all that much what we do," he said, "since none of us is gonna make it off this island alive. Ben Johnson'll see to that."

At dawn the next morning, five weeks to the day after we left Halifax, we struck camp and set off to cross the island. The day was just as nice as it could be, with a warm breeze blowing up from the south and not a cloud in the sky. We made our way through the rocky valley, about three miles, and then onto the snowfield. By this time the sun was high in the sky, and as the day dragged on the snow got softer and softer, until we were sinking up to our knees in slush. Our boots filled with cold water, and the sun burned our faces, and the snow threw off so much glare that our eyes ached. To make things even worse our sledges kept getting bogged down in the slush, and then the whole show would grind to a halt while we dug them out. It wasn't until the sun began to set, around five o'clock, that we finally straggled off the snowfield, sore and sunburned, and made camp on a patch of bare ground near the base of a craggy peak. The professor said we'd only made eight miles.

The next day we did a little better, about nine miles, and after that we had a nice long run of twenty-mile days, with clear skies and mostly easy ground. Every morning at quarter past four the professor would rouse us up, and we'd have to drag ourselves out of our cozy sleeping bags and get ready for another long day of trudging through rocky valleys and over snowy ridges. By five o'clock we'd be underway again.

Four hours later, after hiking through the darkness for what seemed like forever, the sun would finally poke up over the horizon. It would rise to about where the tree line would've been if there'd been one, and then it would glide along the horizon, never getting any higher, until it got around to the other side of the world; then it would slowly sink down out of sight again, and the day would be over.

We crossed all kinds of terrain—mossy tundra, and wide plains, and glistening snowfields, and rocky valleys and high ridges. We had clear skies every day, and it wasn't too cold, except at night, and it didn't ever snow.

Then one day the sky clouded over, and the wind swung around to the north and blew cold; so we knew that snow was coming. Sure enough, along toward noon it did come. It started out as light flurries, but as the afternoon went on the snow came down harder and harder, till by two o'clock it was falling so fast we had almost no visibility. The professor decided to call it a day, so we started to look for a place to camp. We were making our way along a ridgeline when all of a sudden the snow lifted like a curtain—and there was Mount Terror, looming over us. It was just monstrous, with a jagged top and black, broken flanks that reminded me of claws. I could see why they called it Mount Terror.

Even the professor seemed rattled by the sight of it, and he hurried us down off the ridge. A mile from the bottom we found a patch of flat rocky ground near the foot of a jagged peak. It was surrounded by a forest of sharp black rocks that spiked up out of the earth like dragon's teeth. No one liked the looks of the place, but the professor thought we'd be safe from avalanches there, and besides he didn't think we were likely to find a better place. So we made camp. Everybody talked in low voices, and nobody made any more noise than they had to; it was as if there was something huge and scary slumbering close by, and we didn't want to wake it.

I was beat, so I turned in soon after dinner. When I woke again it was dark, and the professor was snoring away in his sleeping bag beside me. The wind was whistling through the rocks, and the tent fluttered and flapped; then an owl went KREK-KREK! KREK-KREK! off in the distance, and something outside the tent fell over and rolled away with a rattle. Soon after that I began to feel drowsy again, and was just starting to drop back to sleep when the most frightening noise I ever heard came ripping out of the darkness—it was like a roar and a scream all mixed up together. I came wide awake—so did the professor—and the next second we were pulling on our boots and parkas and tumbling out of our tent. Everyone else shot out of their tents, too, looking all startled and alarmed, and shined their flashlights into the darkness.

"What in God's name was that?" said Mr. Clark.

"Whatever it was," said Baldy, "God didn't have nuthin' to do with it."

"It was probably a wolf," said Mr. McClintock.

"Wolf, my bum," said Peerless. "That was a polar bear."

"Perhaps," said the professor, "but polar bears rarely come this far inland, and they generally don't hunt at night."

"Do you think it'll come into the camp?" I said.

"No, I don't think so. But we'll set a watch anyway, just to be safe. I'll take the first shift."

So he got his rifle and his pipe and sat down with his back to a boulder while the rest of us went back to bed. I was too worked up to go back to sleep, and for a long time I just lay there, listening to the wind. Finally I heard voices outside; it was Mr. McClintock taking the second watch. Soon after that the professor ducked into the tent and crawled into his sleeping bag. It wasn't too long before he was snoring away; then I drifted off to sleep myself.

Shortly before dawn Mr. McClintock poked his head into our tent and woke us up. He looked worried. The professor rubbed the sleep out of his eyes and asked him what was the matter.

"It's about Bill Turner," Mr. McClintock said.

"Yes," said the professor, "what about him?"

"He's missing."

ATTACKED!

WE got dressed and went outside. And BRRRR! was it ever cold, with the wind fluttering the tents and blowing streaks of snow across the ground. Mr. McClintock took us over to Bill's tent. Peerless and the Sea Leopards were already there, with their caps pulled down over their ears. Mr. McClintock lifted the flap so we could look inside; the tent was empty.

"He probably stepped away from camp during the night, then couldn't find his way back," said Mr. McClintock.

"All right," said the professor. "You, Clark, and Jones each take two men and search in a different direction. Leo, you go south; Jones, east; Clark, west. I'll look to the north. Report back here in one hour. And don't lose sight of this peak; we don't want anyone else getting lost. Is everyone clear? Good, let's get cracking. Orion, you come with me."

He grabbed a flashlight and we headed out. As soon as we got away from the camp we found ourselves in a maze of tall rocks—some as tall as church spires—and I could see how easy it would be to get turned around in the dark and go off in the wrong direction. We called out Bill's name as we went along, but the only answer we heard was the rocks echoing back, BILLLL! BILLLL TURNNERRRR!

About a mile out from the camp we came to a gully. The professor told me to wait at the top while he checked it out, and then he slid down into it and set off along the bottom, calling out Bill's name. I sat on a boulder and watched him until he disappeared around a bend.

As I was sitting there I got to thinking about how nice it would be if the professor found Bill, because then we could take him back to the camp and be heroes. Then I thought, What if *I* found Bill? That would be even better! I pictured how surprised he'd look, sitting against a rock somewhere, all cold and hungry and scared, and how I'd say to him, like nothing was the matter, "Oh, hey, Bill. What are you doing way out here? Breakfast is ready. Let's go." I imagined how everyone would cheer me when I led him into the camp, and crowd around me and tell me how happy they were that I'd come along on the expedition. Well, I got so carried away I forgot I was supposed to stay put, and the next thing I knew I was on my feet and hurrying away to hunt for Bill.

I hadn't gone fifty yards when I came to a little patch of bare ground that was all hemmed in with rocks—and there he was. Or what was left of him, anyway. It only took one glance to see that some kind of animal had killed and eaten him. I'd never seen such a gruesome sight in all my life, and for the next minute or two the world seemed to spin before my eyes. I had to lean on a rock to keep from falling over.

I went back to the gully, feeling all weak and woozy, and when the professor came back I asked him if he'd get mad at me for not staying put if I told him I knew where to find Bill. He said no, he wouldn't; he'd make an exception this time. So I took him to the place and showed him. He looked grim when he saw what had happened to Bill, and he said he was sorry I had to see something like that. I was, too.

We gathered up some rocks and made a little mound over Bill's leftovers. There wasn't any wood to make a cross with, so the professor borrowed my pocketknife and scratched *BT* on a rock and laid it on the mound. Then I took off my cap and looked at my feet while Professor Meriwether said a few words about Bill and his good qualities. I noticed he didn't mention any of the bad ones.

By the time we got back to camp the others had returned from their searches. The news shook everybody up—except Peerless. He just yawned and looked at his watch.

"Was it a wolf that killed him?" said Mr. McClintock.

"I couldn't tell," said the professor. "There were no tracks, and there wasn't enough left of the poor fellow to be able to say what kind of animal killed him. It must've been a polar bear or a wolf, though. There aren't any other animals in the Arctic that could've done that to a man."

"I still say it was a polar bear," Peerless threw in.

"Well, whatever it was, now that we know there are dangerous animals in the area we have to be more careful. From now on we'll set a watch every night, and nobody leaves the camp alone. Especially you, Orion."

He didn't have to worry about *me*; after seeing what that thing did to Bill you couldn't have pried me away from the camp after nightfall.

By that time it was getting lighter, and big flakes of snow were beginning to float down out of the sky. The professor wanted to put a few miles behind us before the weather got worse, so after hurrying through breakfast we packed camp and headed out. We hiked back up to the ridge where we'd first seen Mount Terror, and then we made our way along the ridgeline until we came to a place where the ridge sloped down to a snowfield that stretched away to the north. The slope wasn't steep, so we hopped onto our sledges, and slid down off the ridge and onto the snowfield. It was snowing hard by this time, so the professor had us put on our goggles and rope ourselves together so nobody would get lost. Then off we went, single file, across the snowfield.

We pushed on, with our heads down; and it grew colder and colder, and the wind blew harder and harder, and the snow fell faster. Pretty soon it was a full-blown blizzard, and there was so much snow swirling around that all I could see was the rope running ahead into a solid wall of whiteness.

I was wondering how much worse it could get when all of a sudden something big and scary came charging up out of the blizzard at me. I got a glimpse of a big shaggy head with fiery eyes and a mouth full of fangs; there was a roar and a flash of white, and as I dove to the ground it sprang out of the blizzard and went sailing over me.

The next minute Professor Meriwether came hurrying up and asked me if I was all right. He heard a roar, he said, and started back just in time to see something spring out of the blizzard at me. Everyone else had heard it, too, and they all came running up and wanted to know what it was. I said I didn't know, but I was pretty sure it wasn't friendly.

A sudden roar put a stop to all the jawing. The professor had us circle the sledges, and then he handed out rifles and gave each man a cartridge—just one, because that was all he had. You can bet I wished we had more.

I figured Bill Turner didn't need his rifle now that he was dead, so I asked the professor if I could use it. He asked me if I knew how to shoot; I said yes, my grampa had taught me. So he let me have Bill's rifle. It was a good deal heavier than my grampa's old .22, and the stock was so long I could just barely reach the trigger. The professor watched me draw the bolt back and slot a cartridge into the chamber. He looked satisfied. "You only get one shot," he said. "Make it count."

Then he crouched behind his sledge, with his rifle resting on it, and looked out into the blizzard. Peerless was on the other side of me, talking to his rifle. I couldn't hear what he was saying, but that was all right; I didn't want to know.

The wind was just screaming along now, blowing the snow sideways in great gusts that blotted out everything and left me gasping for air. Between that and my goggles fogging up

I couldn't have hit an elephant if it had been standing right in front of me, let alone a charging wolf or polar bear.

It wasn't long before we realized that whatever had tried to have me for lunch wasn't alone. Between gusts we counted as many as ten of them out there, circling us like sharks. There was so much snow clogging up the air that we couldn't tell what they were, but they were big—bigger than any wolf or polar bear I ever saw, anyway.

Another five minutes dragged by, but it felt more like an hour. I wished they'd go away, or come at us, or something. Anything but this awful waiting!

Suddenly Peerless brought up his rifle. CRACK! goes a shot; then—CRACK! CRACK! CRACK! CRACK!—go four more, one on top of the other, like a string of firecrackers. Next there was a fearsome roar and something came thundering up out of the blizzard at me. My heart shot into my throat, and as I squeezed the trigger of my rifle a noise like a thunderclap went off in my ear; then—BAM!—something slammed into my shoulder and knocked me backwards onto the snow.

"Cease fire!" roared the professor.

But by that time the firing had already stopped. I picked myself up and crawled back to my rifle, with my ear ringing and my shoulder feeling like a horse had just kicked it.

"Did anyone hit anything?" the professor called out.

"Not on this side," said Mr. McClintock. "Three of them charged us, but when we opened fire they vanished back into the blizzard. I've never seen animals move so fast."

"Same over here," said Mr. Clark.

"Remarkable!" said the professor. "It's as if they're trying to get us to use up all of our ammunition."

If that's what they were doing it was working—half of our ammunition was gone. Or that's what I thought, until I saw Peerless taking a box of cartridges out of his backpack.

"You've got more cartridges?" I said.

"Bugger off," he growled. "These are mine."

The professor looked over, and when he spotted the box he said, "For crying out loud, Jones! Why didn't you tell me you had more ammunition? How much do you have?"

Peerless said it was his last box, but you could tell he was lying. The professor snatched his backpack out of his hands and emptied it out onto the snow. Out fell a box of cigars, a pair of dirty undershorts, an old photo of Peerless wrestling a dead crocodile, a signal flare—and about a dozen boxes of ammunition. Peerless turned red.

The professor tossed a box to Mr. Clark and another one to Mr. McClintock; then he gave me another cartridge and took up his position behind his sledge.

Just then another fearsome roar came out of the blizzard, and before I knew what was happening one of the wolves—or bears, or whatever they were—came thundering up out of the snow and sprang right over the sledge barrier. Simon whipped up his rifle, but before he could squeeze off a shot the creature bowled him over and seized him by the throat. The next second a gust of snow swallowed them up.

Then here come the rest of them, all at once, charging in from every side. It was just noise and confusion after that—

nothing but shouts, and roars, and a steady CRACK! CRACK! CRACK! of rifle fire; and the air so full of snow I couldn't see the end of my rifle. Somewhere in all that chaos I caught a glimpse of Peerless tearing off his goggles and firing round after round into the blizzard.

Our situation was desperate. One minute we were firing from behind the safety of our sledges, and the next one of the creatures had broken through our defenses and was ripping and tearing around among us.

Meantime Mr. Clark had swung his rifle around and was taking aim at the creature; it still had Simon by the throat.

"No!" shouted the professor. "You might hit Simon!"

He dropped his rifle, and grabbed an ice axe off his sledge and charged in. He leaped onto the creature's back; the axe flew up; then he brought it crashing back down, burying it all the way up to the hilt in the creature's neck. It let out a roar that turned my insides all to mush, and sprang into the air with a sideways jerk that sent the professor flying off its back. I heard a sickening thud as he landed.

And then it went for him.

I saw I had to do something, so I waved and let out a yell. The creature swung its huge shaggy head around and glared at me. I took aim with my rifle—and then I remembered I hadn't reloaded it yet! The cartridge was still in my hand.

I tried to shove the dang thing into the chamber, but my hands were shaking so much that I dropped it between my knees. I reached down and felt around for it, but I couldn't find it in the snow, and when I looked up again I was staring into a pair of burning red eyes. My heart jammed, and I fell over onto the snow. In another second he was on top of me. I closed my eyes; I didn't want to see myself get eaten, after all. Then I heard a funny hissing noise, followed by a yelp. When I opened my eyes again the creature was gone—and Mr. McClintock was standing over me with a burning flare in his hand.

"Flares!" he roared out. "Use your flares!"

Everyone started setting off flares and hurling them at the creatures. In no time we had a ring of burning flares around us. The creatures skipped and danced around them, roaring and snarling; and then, just like that, they were gone.

We kept the flares going until the blizzard blew itself out a few hours later. Soon after that the sun broke through the clouds—and there was the snowfield, all smooth and white and glistening, stretching away in every direction. Off to the east Mount Terror loomed over us.

As for the creatures, there was no sign of them. No blood, no bodies, no tracks in the snow; nothing.

It was as if they were never there.

HOW I GOT LOST

ALL in all we were pretty lucky; only Simon Killigrew and Professor Meriwether had been injured in the battle. But of those two, Simon was as good as dead. Mr. McClintock did everything he could for him, but that didn't amount to a hill of beans; just holding a dirty rag against his throat was all, while his life drained away. I couldn't stand to watch—it was too sorrowful—so I turned away. When I looked back again the rag was covering his face.

The professor was mostly okay, except two of his ribs had been fractured. Mr. McClintock gave him some pills to ease the pain, and by the time the sun broke through the clouds a few hours later he was up and about again.

I was a little shook up, but all right if you don't count the monster bruise I had on my shoulder. Peerless told me I was lucky I hadn't broken my collarbone. He said it came from not holding my rifle the right way, and then he showed me how. That was all right, I guess; but I still thought he was a slimeball for trying to hog the ammo.

As soon as the professor could walk we put Simon's body on a sledge and set off for Mount Terror to look for a place to hole up for the night. I pulled Simon's sledge with some of the weight taken off, while Awkward Morgan pulled the professor's sledge and his own. Awkward was the biggest and strongest of the Sea Leopards—and the ugliest, too, with a face that looked like a piece of putty with two marbles stuck in it and arms bigger than most people's legs. He was pretty friendly, generally, but you wouldn't want to get him mad.

Mount Terror was a good fifteen miles away, and by the time we straggled up to the line of cliffs that stretched along its western flank the sun was going down. We turned north and made our way along the foot of the cliffs, looking for a place to camp where we'd be safe from attack. After about a mile we came to a break in the cliffs. It was just wide enough to fit the sledges through, but when we got in a little ways it opened out into a space big enough to land a helicopter in, with high cliffs all the way around. We couldn't have found a better spot.

After we put up our tents we took Simon off a little ways and buried him under a mound of rocks. Then everybody pulled off their caps—except Peerless, of course—and Baldy gave a little speech. It was a fine speech, and I'm sure Simon would've appreciated it if he hadn't been dead.

Back at camp Baldy fixed dinner, and everybody sat down around the lantern to eat. We hadn't eaten since breakfast, so we tucked into our food "with a vengeance," as my grampa would say, and for the next little while all you could hear was utensils scraping on plates. Finally Peerless set down his plate and said, "I never knew polar bears were so fast."

"Polar bears don't hunt in packs," said Mr. McClintock. "Those were wolves."

"Wolves, my bum! They were too big."

"Them things wasn't bears," said Baldy, "and with all due respect, sir,"—he nodded to Mr. McClintock—"they wasn't wolves, either. They was hellhounds sent by Ben Johnson to take revenge on us. That's why they didn't leave no tracks."

"There's a simpler explanation for that, Baldy," Professor Meriwether said. "The blizzard blew their tracks away."

"Maybe, but then how come we couldn't kill them? There wasn't a single carcass anywhere to be seen."

"Are you familiar with Occam's razor, Baldy?"

"Ockum's which?"

"Occam's razor. It's the idea that the simplest explanation is usually the right one. In this case the simplest explanation is that any animals we killed or wounded were dragged away by their comrades."

"Hmm," said Baldy. "I still say they was hellhounds."

"And I say they were polar bears," said Peerless.

"They were wolves," said Mr. McClintock.

"The truth is we don't know *what* they are," the professor said. "So until we find out, let's just call them 'bearwolves.'"

That seemed to satisfy Mr. McClintock and Peerless, but Baldy wanted to call them 'hellhound-bearwolves.' Professor Meriwether said that was going too far.

After that Mr. McClintock asked the professor if he still planned to branch off and look for Franklin.

"No, not after what happened this morning," he said. "We have to stay together if we're going to make it off this island alive. We'll head straight up to Cape Deception from here."

Well, Peerless didn't like that at all. He jumped up with his fork in his hand and said, "Hold on, old man! I thought we had a deal. You can't chicken out just because a couple of these yahoos bought the farm."

Mr. McClintock jumped to *his* feet, now, with *his* fork in *his* hand—so did the other Sea Leopards—and for a minute there it looked like Peerless was going to get served. But then the professor stepped between them, and said we'd already had enough bloodshed for one day and would everyone just calm down. He took Peerless off a little ways after that and spoke to him for a few minutes, in private. When they came back Peerless looked as sulky as a bear, and soon afterward he stomped off to his tent.

When it was time to turn in the professor loaded his rifle and took the first watch. Mr. Clark was to take the second watch and Mr. McClintock the third. I slept like a log until dawn, when a commotion woke me up. At first I thought the bearwolves had come back, so I grabbed my rifle and tumbled out of the tent in my long johns. But then I saw that wasn't it at all. It was Mr. McClintock; he was stretched out on the ground with dried blood all over his head and face; he'd been knocked out. The whole camp was in an uproar over it, too. Professor Meriwether was rummaging through the first aid kit, searching for a bandage, while Baldy and the rest of the Sea Leopards ripped and tore around, threatening to do all kinds of awful things to Peerless when they got their hands on him. His tent and sledge were both gone, and so was the professor's backpack, with the dispatch box and map. All of our ammunition was gone, too, except for the one cartridge each of us had in our rifles.

The professor finally found a big enough bandage for Mr. McClintock's head, and then we tucked him into his sleeping bag and lashed him onto a sledge. Professor Meriwether figured that Peerless had about a three-hour head start, and that if we left right away we might be able to catch up to him before dark. All he wanted was to get the ammunition back, he said; he didn't give a hoot about Peerless, and he made the Sea Leopards promise that if we caught him there wouldn't be any violence. They promised; but I noticed that some of them had their fingers crossed.

So we packed up and set off along the cliffs, following the tracks Peerless had left in the snow. It was the dullest, drabbest kind of day, with the sky gloomy and overcast and not a breath of wind to freshen things up. After a few miles the cliffs ended in a snowfield that sloped up the side of Mount Terror, and in the haze ahead we could make out a series of jagged ridges that reached out from the mountain like bony fingers. Peerless's tracks led straight to them.

We spent the rest of that morning and afternoon crossing those ridges; up and down, up and down, one after another until I lost count. Even with his cracked ribs the professor smoked right along. But no one complained, and no one fell back; and at last, around four o'clock, with aching legs and grumbling stomachs, we reached the top of the final ridge. Below us there was a big snowfield, and on the other side of it, about a mile away, we could see a moraine. This moraine sloped down into a foggy valley and was full of boulders.

Suddenly Baldy sang out, "There! On the snowfield!"

I looked. It was Peerless all right, pulling his sledge across the snowfield. He was heading straight for the moraine.

We all forgot how hungry and tired we were, and the next minute we were rushing down off the ridge and making for the moraine as fast as we could haul our sledges. By the time we pulled up to it, an hour later, the fog had crept up from the valley and was beginning to curl around the boulders. It was getting dark, too. But we didn't think about that; all we thought about was catching up to Peerless.

So we didn't stop to rope ourselves together and put our headlamps on like we should have, but just rushed headlong into the moraine, all helter-skelter. The boulders were a lot bigger than they looked from up on the ridge; some were as big as cottages. As we got deeper in among them the snow began to thin out—and along with it Peerless's tracks—until pretty soon the ground was as bare as Mr. Clark's head. Still we pushed on, figuring we'd pick up the tracks again when we came out the other side.

It got darker and darker, and the fog rose higher around the boulders. Before long it was so dim and foggy I began to have trouble seeing the person ahead of me. Well, about that time here comes the tiredness washing over me like a warm bath, and I started to drag. Every so often somebody would pass me and say something like, "Yo! Pick it up, Orion," or, "Come on, Orion. You're falling behind," and I'd give my head a shake and pick up my pace. Then I'd nod off again.

All at once I woke up and found myself standing in front of a boulder; it was as big as an elephant. I looked around, trying to remember where I was. Then it came back to me; I'm in the moraine. It was as quiet as a cemetery, with the fog thicker than ever and giving off a silvery kind of glow in the moonlight. I figured I'd see someone when I got around the boulder, but I didn't; just more boulders. They must be a little further ahead, I thought. So I started off again. Every time I came around a boulder I was certain I'd see someone, but I never did, and after a while I started to get the feeling I was going around in circles. But I couldn't really be sure; everything looked the same in the fog. Finally I stopped and said to myself, I can't keep wandering around like this; I'm only getting more lost. Why didn't I just let out a yell?

So that's what I did.

There! A shout from somewhere off to my right. I let out another yell and set off toward it, feeling better again. The next minute here comes another shout, only this time from my left. Okay, I thought, I'll go *that* way. Well, then I hear a third shout—from *behind* me. Dang it, I thought, how am

I supposed to find them if they keep moving around? Then here comes another shout from my right, and half a second later one from straight ahead. Now I'm all mixed up. Maybe they're spread out all over the place, I thought, searching for me. No, that doesn't make any sense; how would they find one another if they were? Then it hit me—it's the boulders. So I stood still. Sure enough, all the shouts came from the same direction now. They were bouncing off the boulders like pinballs in a pinball machine. I knew I couldn't chase a pinball that was moving at the speed of sound, so I stopped trying. Soon after that the shouts stopped, too.

I wondered what I should do. I had a flare on my sledge; I could shoot it off. Then I thought, No, the fog would just swallow it up. What if I fired my rifle? No, that's no better than a shout. If I had a compass I could head north until I got out into the open. But I didn't have a compass. I *wished* I did, but I might as well have wished to be beamed home. In the end I saw there was nothing I could do but sit tight and wait for the fog to burn off in the morning.

So I unhitched myself from my sledge, and ate a couple of energy bars and drank up the last of my water. Then I sat down with my back against the sledge and stared out into the fog. Before long I began to hear noises coming out of it—or I thought I did, anyway—like little scratchings, and pebbles rolling, and other creepy sounds like that. They spooked me so much that I laid my rifle across my lap, and promised myself that I wouldn't fall asleep, no matter what.

CHAPTER 16

A PUZZLING DISCOVERY

CRACK! went a rifle shot.

I bounced up and looked around. At first I didn't know where I was, or how I got there, or anything; and then I saw the rifle at my feet, and I remembered I was in the moraine. The fog was still pretty thick, but it wasn't nearly as dark as before. It must be getting close to dawn, I thought.

I figured my rifle must've accidentally gone off, but when I picked it up the barrel was cold. So someone else had fired that shot. But why, I wondered? Was the professor trying to signal me? That didn't make any sense; the fog was as heavy as before. Then I thought, Maybe the bearwolves came back and are attacking them. I cocked my head and listened, but I didn't hear any roars off in the distance, or shouts, or rifles going off. I couldn't make it out.

So I stopped worrying about it. There wasn't anything I could do anyway until the fog burned off, and I figured that wouldn't happen for a few more hours. So I jogged around my sledge to warm up, and then I had a couple of chocolate bars and some beef jerky for breakfast. Before long I wished I hadn't eaten that jerky; it made me powerful thirsty, and I didn't have any more water.

Around eleven o'clock the fog began to burn off, and soon after that patches of blue sky appeared overhead. I climbed onto the highest boulder I could find and looked out. A sea of fog stretched away from me in every direction, with the tops of the boulders sticking out of it like little gray islands. There was Mount Terror to the east, as monstrous as ever, and there—wait, is that smoke? It was; a thin line of smoke trailing up into the sky. That's more like it, I thought; they finally found a way to tell me where they are. It cheered me so much that I never thought to ask myself how they could have made the smoke in the first place; there wasn't a single stick of wood or blade of grass on that whole island.

I felt easier now, and I climbed down off the boulder and set out with my sledge. I couldn't see the smoke from down among the boulders, but I saw the sun burning through the fog, and I knew if I kept it on my right I'd come out on the north side of the moraine, near the smoke. I pictured how glad the professor would be to see me, and how glad I'd be to see him. I'd be glad to get some water, too.

By the time I came around the final boulder and stepped into the open the last of the fog had burned off. I stretched and looked around. Off to the north a snowfield swept up toward a rocky ridge, and to the west, along the edge of the moraine, the ground sloped down to a little hill; the smoke was coming from the other side of that hill. It perked me up to see it again, and I headed off toward the hill feeling light and easy. When I got to the bottom of it I called out, "Hey, everybody! It's me!"

I expected to hear shouts come back from the other side, but I didn't; just silence. So I hollered again; nothing. They can't still be asleep, I thought; it's noon. They must've gone back into the moraine to look for me.

So I started up the hill, picturing how surprised they'd all be when they trudged out of the moraine after searching for me all day, only to find me lounging on my sledge with my feet up, like I was never gone! And then I came to the top of the hill—and what I saw on the other side jolted me back to reality. Below me, at the bottom of the hill, there was a black, smoldering mound. It had burned down a little ways, but not so far that I couldn't see what it was made of—our sledges, with our food and gear still on them. Someone had piled them up and set them on fire.

I was floored, it being so different from what I'd expected, and for the longest time I just stood there and stared down at that mound like I was looking at it through a fog. At last a little voice broke through the haze in my head. "You can't just stand up here forever, Orion," it said. "Do something!"

Well, there was only one thing I *could* do, and that was to go down there and try to get to the bottom of it. So I went down the hill, and unhitched my sledge and started to look around. The snow around the fire was all crisscrossed with boot tracks, but that's how it *would* be at a campsite; so that didn't tell me anything. I found boot tracks coming out of the moraine, too, but none going back into it; so I had been wrong about them going back in to search for me. I headed out onto the snowfield next, studying the ground as I went along. Twenty yards away from the fire I came across something that gave me a nasty jolt—a paw print as big around as a basketball, mixed in with the boot tracks. I found another one soon after that; then I saw they were everywhere. A little further out they came together in a line that snaked away to the north. But no boot tracks went off that way. And that wasn't all: I found a little patch of snow soaked with blood. I couldn't make heads or tails of it. It was the strangest and most puzzling thing I'd ever run across.

I tried to work out what had happened. They couldn't have walked away, since there were no boot tracks leading away from the fire. Did they all get eaten by the bearwolves? But there was only that one little patch of blood. If eight grown men had gotten eaten, you'd think there'd be more to show for it. So if they didn't leave on foot, and if they didn't get eaten, then where are they? And who set the sledges on fire? The bearwolves didn't, that was for sure.

Wait a minute—the *fire*. Could they be *in* it?

Cold shivers ran down my back, and I looked over at the mound. If they were in there I had to find out, so I got a ski pole from my sledge and started to poke through the ashes and remains of our gear. Every time I turned over a scorched sledge or lifted up a melted parka I expected to see a charred skull, or a blackened rib cage, or a sooty eyeball staring back at me. But there was no sign of them anywhere, and all I got for my trouble was smoke in my eyes and throat and soot all over my clothes.

Where'd they go? They didn't *fly* away. And whose blood was that? And the rifle shot that woke me up, what was that about? The whole thing beat the pants off me.

Anyway, whatever had happened to the professor and the rest of them, I had to figure out what to do next. But first I had to get some water; I was parched. The mound was still putting out a little heat, so I fished a charred pan out of the ashes and melted some snow in it. I had a long drink, then I filled my water bottles and tied them onto the sledge. After that I sat down and tried to figure out what to do. I knew I couldn't stay there; the bearwolves could come back at any time. I had to go somewhere. But where?

Then it hit me—Peerless! He might still be alive. And if he was, then he could help me find out what happened to Professor Meriwether and the Sea Leopards. But how was I going to find him? I thought and thought, but nothing came to me. Then all of a sudden I hit on the answer. I just had to find out where he came out of the moraine, then follow his tracks until I caught up to him. So I got my sledge and set off along the edge of the moraine. About a quarter of a mile from the fire I came across a set of tracks coming out of the boulders. They led north, over the snowfield.

CHAPTER 16

So I turned north. After a while the snow began to thin out, and not long after that I lost the tracks altogether. All I could do was keep going toward the ridge and hope I could pick up Peerless's tracks on the other side.

An hour later I came to the top of the ridge—and what I saw on the other side made me forget all about Peerless.

Below me there was a valley with a glacier in it—a glacier that was crisscrossed with crevasses. And on the other side of this valley, stretching from the glacier all the way up to the sky, was an enormous laughing devil.

INTO THE VOID

I was scared at first; you bet I was. Coming across a thing like that so sudden and all would've made anybody want to smush down and hide under a rock—except maybe Captain America. But in a minute I saw I didn't have any reason to be scared. It was only a mirage; you could see it shimmering in the afternoon haze. I'd seen them before, in movies, and this one wasn't any different. Only a little scarier, maybe.

Now I knew why Franklin wrote "Laughing Devil" at the end of that trail of X's on his map—the mirage marked the spot where he and his men made their last camp. And that's where I'd find Peerless.

I just had to cross the glacier to get there.

But how am I going to get onto it, I wondered? The foot of the glacier was a wall of ice a hundred feet high, full of deep cracks and overhangs; I couldn't climb it, no way. So I set off along the ridgeline to look for another way onto the glacier. A mile down I came to a place where you could see how the glacier used to butt up against the side of the ridge; all that was left now was a narrow bridge made of ice which went over a gorge. This bridge looked like it might crumble at any minute, but it was the only way I could see to get to the glacier. So I made my way down to it, and then worked up my courage and started across. I took my time about it, too; one step after another, nice and easy. Well, I made it across all right, thank goodness.

By then it was nearly two o'clock. I wanted to get across the glacier before it got dark, so I didn't stop to throw a coil of climbing rope over my shoulder or put on my crampons like I should have. I made good time at first, because I was heading north and the crevasses generally ran parallel to me. But eventually I had to turn east to get to the mirage, and then I had to start crossing over them. If they weren't very wide I could just step over them, but most of the time I had to find a way around them, and that slowed me way down. Then one of my legs suddenly punched through the snow, scaring the daylights out of me, and that's how I found out that crevasses can be hidden under a layer of snow. I got out one of my ski poles after that, and tested the snow ahead of me as I went along. That slowed me down even more.

I was only halfway across the glacier when the sun began to go down. It would've been too risky to keep going in the dark—besides I was bushed—so I looked around for a place to pitch my tent for the night. I spotted one right away, in a kind of hollow between two crevasses, and was just about to unharness my sledge when I noticed a little group of figures moving across the glacier, about a mile away. It's Professor Meriwether, I thought, and the others! I let out a shout and started waving my arms. They turned toward me.

They got bigger every second; it seemed they were galloping right along. They must be excited to find me, I thought. Then I saw them leap over a huge crevasse. What the—?

I stopped waving and got out Collins's old spyglass. Wait a minute, that's not them at all! Those are—bearwolves!

My breath caught, and I whipped around and peeled out of there as fast as I could; which wasn't all that fast, since I had a sledge hitched to me. I was so scared I never thought to slide out of my harness and leave it behind; but as things turned out it was lucky I didn't. I looked over my shoulder as I ran—here they come! a whole pack of them, thundering up in a cloud of snow and snapping their jaws like they hadn't had anything to eat for a month. Before I knew it they were on top of me. The ground rumbled; there was a snarling in my ears, and a blast of hot breath hit the back of my neck.

Then all of a sudden—WHOOSH!—the ground under me dropped away, and I was falling through a shower of snow. The next second something solid came flying up out of nowhere and—SMACK!—everything went black.

When I came to it was as dark as a dungeon. I didn't know where I was, and everything seemed dim and foggy, like I was trying to swim up out of a dream. My head was pounding, and something was tugging on my groin; it felt like someone was giving me a monster wedgie. Something cold was pressing against me, too. I couldn't understand it. Was I dead?

Then the fog in my head began to clear, and it seemed to me that I wasn't dead. If I was, I wouldn't hurt so much.

I got my headlamp out, and switched it on and had a look around. I was in a crevasse. The walls were about seven feet apart and made of ice that was as smooth as glass and hard as concrete. I looked up and saw that my sledge was wedged between them about ten feet above me; I was hanging from it by the short piece of rope that ran from the sledge to my harness—what they call the "tether." Just beyond the sledge I could see a slice of the night sky, sprinkled with stars, but there was no sign of the bearwolves. Then I looked down— except I wished I hadn't! Just the blackest kind of blackness was all, like a gigantic mouth waiting to swallow me up. It scared the breath right out of me, and the next thing I knew I was trying to scramble up the tether and get to the sledge. All of a sudden the rope went limp in my hands, and I had that sickening feeling you get when you're falling; then my harness jerked me to a sudden stop, and as clumps of snow came thumping down on my head something heavy struck my shoulder and then fell away into the darkness below.

For a long time after that I didn't dare to budge. Finally I got the courage to look up. The sledge had skidded deeper into the crevasse; it was now a good twenty feet down from the lip. A coil of climbing rope had come loose in the fall; one end of it was dangling just above my head.

I felt like crying, then. I would have, too, if I'd thought it might help me out of the awful jam I was in. But I couldn't see how it would, so I tried thinking instead.

The first thing I saw was that I couldn't climb back up to the sledge. If I had some ice screws, and my crampons, and ice axes, then maybe I could've done it. But all those things were on the sledge. I couldn't shimmy up the tether, either. I'd tried that already and almost upset the sledge. And even if I could've climbed up to it, then what? I'd still be underneath it. If I tried to climb onto it I'd upset it for sure, and then it would plunge into the crevasse, taking me with it.

Okay, I thought, I can't go up, and unless I want to freeze to death I can't stay here. That means there's only one thing I can do—I have to go *down*. And the only way to do that is by rappelling.

Luckily I had what they call a "belay device" clipped onto my harness, so I *could* rappel. I grabbed the loose end of the climbing rope and pulled it down to me, and then I ran one end through the belay device and tied the other one off to the tether. After that I tied a knot in the free end of the rope. When I had everything cinched up good and tight I used my pocketknife to cut the tether right below where I'd tied the rope to it. My fingers were numb from the cold, so all of that took a long time, and I had to use my teeth a good deal.

Then I began to lower myself down. Right away I had to stop; my harness was putting so much pressure on my groin I couldn't stand it any longer. I was hanging straight up and down; that was the problem. I had to find a way to lean out backwards so I could take the pressure off my groin. I tried pushing away from the wall with my feet, but they just slid around on the ice. Then I found that if I brought my knees up to my chest I could push myself away from the wall—first with my knees, then my feet—until I was horizontal. It was the scariest kind of feeling, leaning out over empty space like that, backwards and with no wall to hug. But at least I was comfortable.

I started down again. Pretty soon I couldn't see the sledge any more; just the rope running up into the darkness.

Down, down, down I went, into the void.

Then I felt the knot hit against my hand, and I stopped. I *had* to stop—I was at the end of the rope. And I still hadn't reached the bottom yet!

I was stunned. I'd never thought the rope wouldn't reach to the bottom. It was 150 feet long, after all. A shudder went through me, and I thought, What if there *is* no bottom?

I could feel the cold creeping into me as I wondered what to do. I knew I'd freeze to death if I didn't do something soon. But what? I couldn't climb back up, and I couldn't go down, either, not unless— No! I could never do *that*, not in a million years. I'd rather freeze to death.

So I just dangled there at the end of that rope until I *did* begin to freeze to death. And then I got out my pocketknife and did what I thought I'd never do in a million years—

I cut the rope.

CHAPTER 18

HOW I ALMOST GOT EATEN

I'D just started to fall when—WHUMP!—I landed on something soft. It was a big mound of snow. I couldn't believe it. One minute I'm falling, the next I'm not!

I tried to stand up, but my legs were too numb. I rubbed them until I could feel them again, and then I stood up and looked around. I was in a kind of alley, with glistening blue walls that soared straight up into the darkness and a sloping floor made of ice. It was as silent as a tomb. I saw my rifle sticking out of the snow and pulled it out. I had two bruises on my shoulder now, and both were from that stupid rifle.

Then I set off in the direction that sloped upward. After a little while I came to a fork. The left branch went down; the right branch sloped up. I took the right one. It went up for about fifty yards, then dead-ended. So back I went and took the other branch. I followed it—all the while going down—until I came to a kind of stairway that went down into the darkness. I made my way down it. At the bottom I came to a cavern that was as big as a church. It had a ledge running along the outside and a giant black hole in the middle that looked as if it went all the way to the center of the earth. I made my way along the ledge, hugging the wall and trying not to look down. I found passages leading away, but most of them were too narrow for me to fit through, and the rest sloped down or had floors made of rotten ice. I didn't want to think about what would happen if I fell through one.

I'd gone almost all the way around when I came across a passage that didn't slope down or have a rotten floor. Forty feet into it I came to a three-way fork. One of the branches sloped up, so I took that one. Well, pretty soon here I come to another fork, then another one after that. Next I knew I was in a kind of maze, with forks at every turn and passages branching off from other passages every which way. Some of the passages were so broad I couldn't see the walls; others were so narrow I'd have to take off my knapsack to squeeze through. After a while I came to a place that looked familiar; it seemed as if I might have been there before. So I got out my pocketknife and began to scratch arrows in the walls. At least I wouldn't be going around in circles now.

On I went, up one passage and down another. Every time I came to an arrow I wouldn't go that way, but made a new arrow and went the new way. Well, after wandering around for I don't know how long, here I come to a place that's got five passages branching off from it—and every one of them was marked with an arrow!

I gave up, then. I was hungry, and thirsty, and exhausted. To top it all off I was lost inside a glacier!

I dropped my rifle and knapsack and sat down. It felt ever so good to be off my feet, and I figured it would be all right if I closed my eyes for a minute. Only a minute, I promised myself; then I'd get back up and find my way out.

Well, I must've had my eyes closed for a lot longer than a minute, because when I woke up I was stiffer than a board. It was pitch black, too. I switched on my headlamp, but the light didn't come on. I tried it again; nothing. A scare shot through me, and I tried to remember if I'd shut it off before I took my nap; I don't think I had. The batteries must have run down while I slept—and I didn't have any spares!

I felt sick.

How am I ever going to find my way out of here without any light, I wondered? I'm not, that's how. Then here comes that little voice in my head again, saying, "Stop feeling sorry for yourself, Orion, and get up off your rear end! Just think how mad your grampa will be if you die down here."

So I rubbed my legs until I could move them again, then picked up my things and set off into the darkness. I put my hand on a wall to guide me.

I wandered around in that awful darkness until I couldn't remember a time when it wasn't dark; it seemed as though it always had been dark, and always would be. As the hours passed I began to lose hope. All I wanted to do was curl up on the ice and go to sleep. But whenever I was about to that pesky voice said, "Don't you do it, Orion! If you die down here your grampa will ground you for the rest of your life."

So I stumbled on. And on, and on, and on.

Then—what's this? Is the floor sloping *up*? I didn't dare hope, because if it turned back down I knew I'd just curl up on the ice and go to sleep forever. But it didn't turn down, and before long I began to make out the walls. Wait—is that a light up ahead? I dropped my rifle and stumbled toward it. The light got brighter; I turned a corner—and there, at the end of a kind of cul-de-sac, I saw a bright beam of sunlight flooding through a hole at the top of a snowbank. I clawed my way up the bank, and when I pushed my head through the hole there was the clear blue sky above me, and the sun just shining away in it!

I went back for my rifle, and then I climbed out through the hole and let the sun warm my body. I wanted to sleep, but my thirst wouldn't let me. While I was lost inside the glacier all I could think about was finding my way out; now that I was out all I could think about was how thirsty I was. I had to find water.

I looked around. I was in a kind of forest, except the trees looked like giant Popsicles and were made of ice instead of wood; I figured they'd broken off the back of the glacier as it passed through the valley. All I could do was start walking and hope I found water, so I got my things and set off.

I walked all morning. Around noon I sat down on a rock to rest, but pretty soon my thirst got to torturing me so bad

I had to get up and start walking again. The ice forest was perfectly still and quiet; the only sound I could hear was the crunching of my boots on the snow.

Well, I was crunching along, wondering if there was any chance that I might come across a drinking fountain, when all at once I thought I heard a noise. I stopped and listened for a minute, but I didn't hear a thing; just the stillest kind of silence. I must have imagined it, I thought. So off I went again—CRUNCH! CRUNCH! CRUNCH!—over the snow.

Then I heard it again—only this time I was sure about it. It had come from behind me, so I turned around, nice and easy—and there he was, glaring at me from among the ice trees. I hadn't had a good look at a bearwolf until then, and I saw that he wasn't a polar bear *or* a wolf, but something in between. He was just monstrous—as big as a horse—and he had the wickedest fangs I ever saw; a saber-toothed tiger was nothing compared to *him*. He just stood there, with slobber dripping out of his mouth, and glared at me. I could tell he was thinking about having me for lunch.

I was so scared I almost forgot I had a rifle. I slung it off my shoulder, ever so slowly, and pulled off my mitts one at a time with my teeth. My hands were purple from frostbite.

The bearwolf let out a growl. I brought up my rifle, and then took aim and pushed against the trigger with the back of my thumb. I felt it give a little, then—CLICK!

I'd forgotten to take the safety off!

The bearwolf let out a roar and charged at me. I dropped the rifle and tried to run, but my feet got tangled up, and as he sprang at me I went over backwards onto the snow. He went sailing over me, so close I felt a rush of wind; then he landed like a cat and wheeled around. Here he comes again! I shut my eyes and waited for his jaws to close over my head; there was nothing else I *could* do. Then—

BANG! went a gun, and the ground shook with a crash.

I opened my eyes. The bearwolf was stretched out on the ground inches from my head, and there was something dark oozing out of him onto the snow. It was blood.

The next minute here come nine or ten men riding out of the ice forest—on bearwolves! Their clothes were white and sparkly, and they wore balaclavas and carried muskets.

Three of them got down from their bearwolves and came up to me. One was tall and burly; one was short and thick; the third had a doctor's bag. The man with the doctor's bag looked me over while the other two watched. When he was done he pulled off his balaclava—so did the other two—and didn't I get a surprise then! For the tall man was none other than Goggly Eyes, and the short one was Colonel Gore. I'd never seen the third man before. He looked around forty or so, and wore glasses and had an easygoing kind of face.

"Confound you, boy!" said Goggly Eyes. "Don't you think I have far more important things to be doing with my time than hunting for lost children?" Then he says to the doctor, "Well, Little? Is he going to live, or shall I order the men to prepare a grave?"

"That won't be necessary," said Dr. Little. "His hands are badly frostbitten, and he's dehydrated—but he'll live."

Goggly Eyes looked disappointed. "I see," he said. "Well, do what you have to then, but be quick about. Her ladyship is expecting me for dinner soon."

Dr. Little took a bottle and a dropper out of his bag and put a few drops of medicine on my tongue. Soon my head began to feel heavy; then the world got dimmer and started to close in around me, until all I could see was Goggly Eyes standing over me. I tried to ask him who he was, but I just couldn't seem to get my mouth to work.

"What are you trying to say, boy?" he said. "Do you want to know who I am? Is that it?"

I nodded, and the last thing I remember before I sank into the darkness was Goggly Eyes telling me who he was.

"My name," he said, "is John Franklin."

DOCTOR LITTLE

"OH, you're awake!" somebody said.

I opened my eyes. I was in a bedroom, it seemed. It was a regular bedroom, only old-fashioned; everything looked all faded and washed out. Besides the bed there was a little white dresser with a basin of water on it for washing your face in, and a wicker chair with a pair of shiny black shoes and a new set of clothes on the seat, and a rocking chair. This rocking chair had a lady in it. She had a round face with shiny little eyes and a pile of knitting on her lap.

"Oh, you poor thing!" she said. "I've been ever so worried about you. Why, I was starting to wonder if you'd wake up at all! Mrs. Darlington—that's my sister, dear—anyway, she stopped by the other day to get some roly-polies, and when she saw you she said— Well, maybe I won't trouble you with what she said just now, because it's been three days since the doctor brought you here, and you must be *dreadfully* hungry, you poor lost lamb!"

Before I could say I was she snatched up her knitting and went sailing out of the room. I couldn't understand it. Had they got me back to Halifax somehow? Who was that lady? And what was I doing in somebody's house, anyway? You'd think they would've at least taken me to a hospital.

I tried to remember what had happened in the ice forest, but it all seemed so far away and hazy, like a dream you can only remember snatches of. I remembered a bearwolf, and a loud bang, and men wearing sparkly white clothes. Weren't they riding bearwolves, too? No, that couldn't be right. And wasn't one of them a doctor? Dr. Little—that was it. Wasn't Goggly Eyes there, too? And didn't he tell me his name was John Franklin? That couldn't be right, either. Franklin lived way back in the nineteenth century; he had to be long dead by now. Had it all just been a dream?

Well, just when I'd made up my mind that it *had* been a dream, the door opened and in walked Dr. Little himself.

"How's my patient this evening?" he said.

"I'm all right," I said, staring at him.

"I imagine you're rather hungry."

I said I was. He laughed and said, "Then you'll be pleased to know that Mrs. Jopson will be back soon with your supper. She's been at your side since the moment you arrived here, waiting for you to wake up so she could stuff you full of her cooking. Now, shall we have a look at you?"

I said all right, so he sat down on the bed and had a look at me. My hands and feet were wrapped up in bandages, and when he got done peering down my throat and rummaging around in my ears he started to take them off. I was so sure he'd cut off all my fingers and toes because of the frostbite that I couldn't watch. But after a minute I saw I was wrong. There were my fingers, all ten of them, and as good as new; same with my toes. I could hardly believe it.

"I see that you're surprised," he said with a laugh. "And you should be. That medicine I gave you back in the ice forest is the only known cure for acute frostbite. It's a pity it can't be shared with the rest of the world."

"Why not?" I said.

"Oh, it's all rather complicated, I dare say. The important thing is, you still have your fingers and toes. Well, I should let you rest. Perhaps I'll see you in the morning."

"Wait! Where am I?"

"Ah. That's also rather complicated. For now let's just say that you're in a house."

Well, that didn't tell me anything I didn't already know. I asked him if the house was in Halifax.

"Halifax? Whatever gave you that idea, my dear boy? I'm afraid you're a very long way from Halifax."

"So where am I, then?"

He looked like he was about to tell me. But then he said, "I promise I'll answer all of your questions soon. You're still weak, and some of what I have to tell you might come as a shock. It would be better to wait until you're stronger."

Better for him maybe, but not for me. Now that he'd gone and gotten my curiosity up, I wouldn't be able to sleep until I learned everything. So I said, "But I *am* stronger. Can't you tell me now?"

"No, I really think—"

At that moment the door flew open, and here comes Mrs. Jopson sailing back in with my supper. "Here you go, dear!" she sang out. "I fixed you something special—potted meat, bashed neeps, baby seal's face drowned in lichen sauce, and the doctor's personal favorite: sea-elephant pudding!"

I really was a long way from Halifax. But it didn't matter; I was so hungry I would've eaten an old shoe.

Dr. Little started toward the door, but I couldn't let him leave me like that, all curious and wondering, so I asked him to stay and tell me everything while I ate my supper, and not make me wait. At first he didn't want to; he said it might set me back. Then Mrs. Jopson said, "Oh, Doctor, just tell the poor dear. He won't be able to rest until you do. You know how curious children are. Why, my sister, Mrs. Darling—"

"All right!" said the doctor. "I surrender."

So after Mrs. Jopson left he sat down in the rocking chair and took a hankie out of his pocket and polished his glasses while I started on my supper. After a minute he says, "What would you say if I told you that we're still on the island?"

"You mean there's a house up here?" I said.

"More than a house. A colony. An entire *city*, really."

"A city! But that's impossible."

"Why is it impossible?"

I tried to think of a reason why there couldn't be a city on a frozen island at the top of the world, but I couldn't come up with one. It just didn't *seem* possible.

"How come nobody knows about it?" I said.

"The people who live here do," said the doctor.

"I mean the people who don't live here."

"Ah. That's because the man in charge doesn't want them to. His predecessors didn't, either."

"Who's the man in charge?"

"You met him in the ice forest. His name is Franklin."

"But how can that be? I thought Franklin lived back in the nineteenth century. Wouldn't he be dead by now?"

Dr. Little laughed. "You're thinking of a different man," he said. "The John Franklin you're thinking of is the famous explorer who founded this colony. He's been dead for over a century now. The man you met is his great-great-grandson, John Franklin the Fifth."

Then he went on and told me the history of the colony, which they called New London. He told how the first John Franklin founded it back in 1847 to get away from all the wars they were always getting themselves into over there in Europe, and how three-quarters of the men who came with him died of cold and hunger (I thought about the skeleton in the cave when he said that). Then he explained how they built the city using stone they quarried from Mount Terror, and how they mined coal to heat their houses, and hunted seals and whales and grew vegetables in water, and sailed to Greenland and brought back wives, and how over the years so many of them lost their fingers and toes to frostbite that their scientists decided to find a cure for it, and did. Finally he explained how they crossed polar bears with wolves and got bearwolves, to keep people out.

"Unfortunately," he said, "they also keep people in."

"You mean nobody can leave?"

He looked at his watch. "I think we've talked long enough for now," he said. "It's almost midnight."

"But you said you'd answer all my questions."

He laughed and said I could ask one more. So I asked him about the mirage. He said it was entirely natural, and made by sunlight bouncing off the glacier; it was just a coincidence that it looked like a devil. One of the reasons the first John Franklin put the colony where he did, he said, was because he thought the mirage would scare people away.

Then he got up. "I really must let you rest now," he said. "Perhaps I'll see you in the morning. Good night."

But I didn't see him in the morning, or in the afternoon or evening, either. I didn't see him at all that day. Same the next day, and the next one after that. Every day he left the house before the sun came up and didn't come home until after I went to bed; Mrs. Jopson said he had lots of patients to see. I was itching to go outside and explore the city, and meet the people and see what they were like, but Mrs. Jopson said I had to stay in the house until Dr. Little was satisfied that I'd recovered. So I stayed in the house.

It was an interesting house they had there. It was tall and skinny, and squeezed in between two other houses just like it in a long row of houses that stretched from one end of the block to the other. It had creaky stairs, and narrow hallways and bathtubs with feet. There were three floors and an attic. They called the first floor the *ground* floor, and the second floor the *first* floor, and the third floor the *second* floor. It made no sense, but that's what they did.

The kitchen was at the back, looking over an alley, and it always had delicious smells coming out of it. Dr. Little had his own study, and across the hall from it was a room they called the drawing room; only I never saw anybody drawing in there. It had a dark green sofa in it, and two armchairs, and a funny-looking piano that nobody knew how to play. On top of this piano there was a shiny white vase that had a picture on it of two sparrows, or whatever they were, standing on the edge of a fountain with red roses growing around them. There was a fireplace in there, too. It had a painting above it of a handsome young man in a naval uniform, and behind him you could see a tall ship trapped in the ice. At the bottom of this painting there was a brass plate that said *Thomas Jopson, Captain's Steward*, and every morning Mrs. Jopson would come in and polish that plate until it shined. In the evenings she would light a coal fire in the fireplace and make me sit across from her while she knitted and told me the latest gossip about Mrs. Hornby and the other ladies in her little group of ladies. After about five minutes of that I'd be wishing I was back in the crevasse.

Three days went by. Then one morning I came down for breakfast and found Dr. Little waiting for me at the table. It was the first time I'd seen him since that first night, and I wanted to ask him if he knew anything about the professor and my other friends. So after we said good morning to one another I explained how I'd come to the island with friends, and asked him if he knew anything about them.

"As it happens, I do," he said. "In fact, that's why I'm still here. I wanted to know if you'd like to go see them."

"You mean they're still alive?"

"Very much so. And they're rather anxious to see you."

"Well, let's go! Where are they? Is it far?"

"No, not very. But I must prepare you first."

"What do you mean?"

A grim look came over his face, and he said, "I'm sorry I have to tell you this, Orion, but your friends are in prison."

"Prison! What for?"

"Murder."

WORMWOOD PRISON

MURDER! Not Professor Meriwether, I thought; no way. Not any of them. Who'd they murder, anyway? Peerless?

I had to find out, so I asked Dr. Little how soon we could leave for the prison. He said as soon as I had my breakfast. There were some roly-polies on the table, so I popped one into my mouth and dropped another one in my pocket, and said I had my breakfast. Dr. Little laughed, and we put our coats on and headed out.

I'd never seen such a strange and wonderful city. On every corner there were hawkers selling flummery, and plum-duff and other things I never heard of, and boys with bundles of newspapers at their feet singing out, "Extra! Extra! Read all about it! Murder on Lower Slag Lane!", and steam carriages chugging up and down the street. Dr. Little waved one down and we set off for the prison. Along the way we passed the strangest kinds of houses and the oddest kinds of shops, and people in funny clothes. All the ladies wore humongous hats with feathers on them and had umbrellas even though there wasn't a single cloud in the sky; the men wore hats shaped like giant soup cans and carried walking sticks with handles made of walrus teeth. When one of them met a lady he knew he would bow and say, "Good morning to you, Miss Jones." Then the lady, she would drop a little curtsey and say, "And to you, Mr. Smith." They were awful polite, those people.

A few blocks from the doctor's house we came to a park. It had trees and people walking their dogs in it just like any old park, only the trees weren't like any I'd ever seen before; they were the softest kind of blue and had spikey leaves that sparkled in the sun. On the other side of this park there was a marble building called a mausoleum where they kept what was left of the first John Franklin, and just beyond that was a bridge that went over a huge crack in the earth. This crack was wider than a football field and so deep you couldn't see the bottom of it. On the other side were rundown buildings and narrow, crooked streets that were crowded with people. These people weren't anything like the polite ones; they had grimy faces and bent backs. Dr. Little said that part of town was called Cheapside. He told me never to go there alone.

About a mile and a half from the park we passed a courthouse with a clock tower on it that they called Little Ben, and soon after that we arrived at the prison. It was an ugly building with an iron gate that said *Wormwood Prison* over it. A guard let us in and took us to the warden's office. The warden was sitting at his desk, hunched over behind a stack of papers that was so high all I could see of him was the top of his bald head. He didn't look up when we came in, but just grumbled and said, "Yes? What is it now?"

"It's Dr. Little, sir," said the guard.

The warden peered at us over the stack of papers. He had a thin, scraggly face and a chin that looked like the toe of an old boot. He looked me over, all suspicious-like, and said, "What's this, Little? You know the rules—no visitors."

"This young man is one of the Outsiders," said Dr. Little. "He came to see his friends."

"I don't care why he came. No visitors!"

"Warden, this boy has had a severe shock. It's essential to his recovery that he see his friends."

"Is that so? The little urchin don't look sick to me."

"Are you a doctor, sir?"

"You know I'm not."

"Then kindly refrain from offering medical opinions," said Dr. Little, pretty sharp. "Now unless you want to explain to His Lordship why you put this boy's health at risk, I suggest you reconsider."

The warden gave Dr. Little the blackest kind of look; then he turned back to his papers and grumbled to the guard that I could go with the doctor on his rounds.

I almost wish he hadn't. Take the darkest, dirtiest, noisiest, most foul-smelling place you can imagine and multiple it by ten—and that's Wormwood Prison. The cells were cold, and damp, and slimy, and filled to bursting with prisoners; they even had whole families living in there, with their pets and furniture and everything. The smell was so awful I had to hold a hankie over my nose.

The guard held out a lantern and led us along the dank, narrow corridors, stopping every so often to unlock a cell so Dr. Little could go inside and look at someone who was sick or hurt. Once I followed him in. There was a boy in there who'd gotten one of his fingers broken by a policeman. He looked about my age and was so bony that his clothes hung from him like drapes. I felt sorry for him, so I gave him the roly-poly I had in my pocket.

After a while we came to a cell that was different from all the others: it had a solid iron door. The guard let us in and locked the door behind us. In the gloom I could make out seven or eight men sitting with their backs against the walls or stretched out on the floor. One of them got up to his feet and shuffled over to us. I didn't recognize him at first, there being so much grime on his face; then I saw it was Professor Meriwether. He looked about forty years older than the last time I'd seen him.

His face lit up when he saw me, and he took my hand in his, and shook it and said how glad he was to see me. Then everyone else got up and shuffled over, and shook my hand the same way and said how glad *they* were to see me, too. I said I was glad to see them and find out they weren't dead, because until an hour ago I'd thought they probably were.

Of course they wanted to hear my story—they all did—so

while Dr. Little changed the bandage on Mr. McClintock's head I told them everything that happened from the time I got lost in the moraine to when I woke up four days later to find Mrs. Jopson chattering away at me. And when I got to the part where I was dangling at the end of the rope in the crevasse, with my pocketknife in my hand, even the doctor stopped what he was doing; and everybody leaned in, and it got so quiet you could've heard a mouse breathing.

"Well," the professor said when I came to the end, "I can only hope that your grandfather doesn't hear that story. He'd never let me take you anywhere again. Ha, ha, ha!"

Then he told me *their* story. It seemed no one knew I was lost until they heard my shout, and when they realized they couldn't find me in the fog the professor decided to set up camp outside the moraine and try to signal me with a flare in the morning. He didn't sleep at all that night, he said; he blamed himself for rushing into the moraine without taking precautions to make sure no one got lost. As for Peerless, he said, nobody cared about him any more.

The next morning the professor was up at dawn.

"And that's when it happened," he said.

"When what happened?" I said.

"The accident that landed us here. And, I'm sorry to say, also cost a man his life."

"Tell me about it."

"There isn't much to tell, really. I'd just stepped out of my tent when I saw a bearwolf coming out of the fog. I fired at it immediately, of course. I had no idea there was a man on it, and to tell the truth I'm not sure I would've believed my eyes even if I had seen him. Anyway, I hit the poor fellow in the leg. We did all we could for him, but the bullet had hit one of his arteries, and— Well, we couldn't save him."

"Who was he?"

"I believe his name was Gibson."

"Gibson! He was at my house. He got shot there, too. So what happened next?"

"Well, within a few minutes of my rifle going off we were surrounded by about twenty men, all of them mounted on bearwolves and armed with muskets. They set our sledges on fire, and then tied us all up, threw us over the backs of their bearwolves, and brought us here. I'm sure you can imagine how worried we were about you. It wasn't until the doctor here came to check on us the next day that I was able to get them to send out a search party."

"So what happens now?"

"It seems we're going to be put on trial. We've even been given our own attorney. I'm not really sure what to make of him, though. He's a bit of an odd duck."

"But it was just an accident!" I said. "I can't believe they're going to put you on trial."

"Well, Orion," said the professor, "you better get used to the idea, because the trial is tomorrow."

THE TRIAL

THE next morning at half past nine me and Dr. Little and Mrs. Jopson got into a steam carriage and headed down to the courthouse. All of the houses and shops were closed up, and except for a few dragoons patrolling here and there the streets were empty. When we got to the courthouse I found out why—the whole town had turned out for the trial. You could see people streaming in from every direction, some in the dandiest getups, others in shabby secondhand coats and drooping hats. People were crowding up the courthouse steps and jostling each other to get inside, and the sidewalks were lined with hawkers selling lemon cakes and ginger-beer, and paperboys singing out, "Extra! Extra! Read all about it! Trial of the century! Only in the *Daily Blizzard*!", and fire-eaters and jugglers for the kids. It was something else.

We went up the steps with the other people and crowded into the courtroom. It was just like your regular courtroom, except it had five chairs behind the judge's bench instead of one, and up against one side there was a big iron cage with a door at the back. It was hot, and noisy, and crowded; but everybody was in a good mood, and the people were as nice as they could be. Whenever any of them noticed Dr. Little they'd shake his hand and thank him for whatever it was he did for their little Mary, or Elizabeth, or Edward, or George or whoever it was. And when we couldn't find seats some of the ladies made their husbands give up theirs.

At ten o'clock a door opened and in marched a man with a chest as big around as a barrel. He was decked out in the most outlandish costume, with peacock feathers and panty hose, and he carried a staff with a golden lion's head on it. He banged it on the floor three times and boomed, "All rise!" So we all rised. Next here come the judges filing in. Franklin was the chief one. He had on a long black gown and the most comical wig I ever saw; it was white and curly. So did the other judges. And didn't they all look sour, too!

After they got seated and comfortable Franklin banged his gavel and ordered the bailiffs to bring in the accused. One of the bailiffs opened the door at the back of the cage, and the next minute in shuffled Professor Meriwether, shackled hand and foot. Mr. McClintock and the rest of the Sea Leopards shuffled in after him, with Mr. Clark bringing up the rear. I could tell he wanted to polish his head, but with his hands in chains he couldn't get to his rag.

There was a ruckus among the people when they came in, and Franklin had to bang his gavel a couple of times to get everybody to quiet down. Then he told the clerk—his name was Mr. Honey—to read the charges. So Mr. Honey picked up piece of paper, and said, "Leo McClintock, James Clark, Baldy Brownlow, Awkward Morgan, Charlie Button, Cam Hoffer, and Corky Fleck,"—those were the Sea Leopards—"you are hereby charged with trespassing upon the sovereign territory of New Britain, possessing firearms, espionage, and accessory to murder. How do you plead?"

Nobody said anything.

"I say," Mr. Honey repeated, "how do you plead?"

Still nobody said anything.

"I say there, how do you fellows plea—"

"Aww, go suck an egg!" said Baldy.

And then he flipped off the judges.

Everybody looked puzzled, and turned to their neighbors and asked them what it meant. Nobody seemed to know, so Mrs. Jopson leaned over and asked me. I couldn't think of a polite way to explain it, so I just blurted it out. She turned as red as a cherry; so did the doctor. Of course Mrs. Jopson had to tell the lady next to her, and *she* had to tell the one next to *her*—and before you could say "cheese and crackers" the whole courtroom knew what it meant. And didn't the people carry on then! Franklin had to hammer his gavel for a whole minute before they settled back down.

When it was finally quiet again he ordered Mr. Honey to continue reading out the charges. So Mr. Honey cleared his throat and said, "Charles Meriwether, you are charged with the aforementioned crimes, as well as the crime of murder. How do you plead?"

The professor didn't plead at all. He just stood there, tall and proud, and said, "My associates and I refuse to recognize the authority of this court, and, furthermore, we demand to be set free at once!"

There was another brouhaha among the people, then, and I could see they were glad they came. The judges sitting on either side of Franklin looked at one another; it seemed they weren't used to troublesome prisoners.

Franklin, of course, had another one of his tantrums.

"Order, confound it!" he thundered. "By Gad, I *will* have order in my courtroom! If the accused refuse to enter a plea, their attorney will enter one for them. What will it be?"

Silence.

"Confound it! I said 'What will it be?'"

"He isn't here, my lord," said Mr. Honey.

"*Who* isn't here?"

"The attorney for the accused, my lord. Mr. Diggle."

"Confound it, Honey! Where is he?"

"I don't know, my lord. I haven't seen him today."

"Well, go and find him, you—"

Just then the doors burst open, and a funny-looking little man in an unbuttoned gown and a wig that was too small for his head came scurrying in with an armful of papers. "I beg your forgiveness, m'lords," he said. "The coachman—"

"Confound you, Diggle!" said Franklin. "This is the fifth

time this month you've been late for one of my trials."

"I'm sorry, m'lord. It was the coachman's fault, I assure you. He wanted an extra shilling for opening the top, which I never asked him to do, but the silly fellow insisted. So I set my papers on the seat—to get a shilling out of my purse, you know—and by the time I realized I'd left them there the silly fellow had driven off! I went to the carriage office, but they said they could do nothing unless I had the license number. Well, I knew it began with a two and ended with a six—no, that's not right. It began with a six and ended with a—"

"Diggle!" Franklin boomed.

"Yes, m'lord?"

"How do your clients plead?"

"Plead, m'lord?"

"Yes, plead. Your clients refuse to plead."

"They refuse, m'lord?"

"Yes, confound you! They refuse to plead! Which part of that don't you understand, you silly boob? You must enter a plea for them. Well, what will it be?"

"One moment, m'lord," said Diggle.

He started rummaging through his files and muttering to himself, but it was so quiet that we could hear every word he said. "No," he says, "that's the Thompson case. What about this one? Oh! Those are the receipts from my hairdresser. I wondered where they'd gone." Then he says, "Ah, here it is! Yes, that's what I thought. We plead 'not guilty,' m'lord."

Franklin looked ready to blow. But he just sighed and said, "The prosecutor for the Crown may put on his case."

THE TRIAL

So the prosecutor got up and put on his case. Shanks was his name, Silas Q. Shanks; and I never saw a sneakier, slicker, shiftier character—except Peerless. It was amazing how he could turn facts upside down and make everyone believe that a thing was the opposite of what it really was. He was a true lawyer, Shanks.

Well, he was clipping along, making the professor sound like a cold-blooded murderer, when all at once he stops and says, "But why should I go on? You needn't take *my* word for any of this, gentlemen of the jury. There's a witness!"

A gasp went up from the courtroom, and everyone leaned forward and stretched out their necks to see over the people in front of them. I did, too; I couldn't wait to see who the witness was. Well, who waltzes in but Peerless! He had on a flashy new outfit with silver buttons and gold cuff links, and as he stepped into the witness box he saw me in the crowd and gave me a wink, as if we were the best of buddies!

He swore on a Bible—they could've used a dictionary for all the good it did—and then Shanks had him tell the jury how he'd been hiding behind a boulder when the shooting happened, and how he'd seen Gibson trot up on his bearwolf and tip his hat to the professor and say howdy, and how the professor brought up his rifle anyway, and how Gibson said he had a wife and five kids and begged the professor not to shoot, and the professor said he didn't care if he had fifty and shot him anyway. After that one of the bailiffs brought out Professor Meriwether's rifle and showed it to the jury while Peerless testified that it was the same rifle the professor shot

Gibson with. That part was true, technically, but everything else was lies—and the jury ate it right up.

Then Shanks had Peerless tell the jury how I got the map from Henry Collins. After that Shanks said, "Gentlemen of the jury, Henry Collins is a name that is no doubt familiar to you—he was the scoundrel who stole the Founder's map and fled in the *Lady Jane*. Why did he commit these crimes? Because he wanted to betray the secret of our colony to the world. Henry Collins was not only a thief, but a traitor!"

"You lie!" someone yelled.

I looked around. There was a girl standing up a few rows behind me, and she was glaring at Shanks like she was trying to burn a hole through him with her eyes. She was my age, and had freckles and red hair. I was sure I'd seen her before, but I didn't know where. Meanwhile Franklin had a fit and ordered the bailiffs to remove her. She didn't go quietly.

After she was gone Shanks turned the witness over to Mr. Diggle. He asked Peerless a few questions that had nothing to do with anything; then he rummaged through his papers, and scratched his head, and dropped his pencil, and crawled under the table to look for it. At that point Franklin lost his patience and told him to sit down.

Then the jury filed out. Five minutes later they filed back in. The foreman handed a slip of paper to Mr. Honey, and Mr. Honey passed it to Franklin. Franklin read the verdict:

"On the charge of espionage, the jury finds the accused—*innocent*. On the remaining charges, including the charge of murder, the jury finds the accused—*guilty*."

Most of the people jumped up and cheered; but some of them didn't, and Dr. Little and Mrs. Jopson were among the ones who didn't. Franklin banged his gavel until it was quiet again; and then he said, in the grimmest kind of voice:

"For your crimes against the people of New Britain, you are hereafter banished. On the day after tomorrow, at dawn, you shall be taken out to the Valley of Crevasses, where you shall be left without food or shelter—*until you be dead*. May God have mercy on your souls."

THE MIDNIGHT MEETING

MY head was spinning all the way back to Dr. Little's house. I don't remember leaving the courtroom, or getting into the carriage, or the ride back or anything. It wasn't until we were in the hallway and taking off our coats that I knew where I was again. And the first thing I said was, "He can't do that!"

"I'm afraid he can," said Dr. Little. "Franklin has absolute power here. His word is the law."

"But isn't there something we can do? There's got to be."

"Mrs. Jopson, would you kindly make us some tea?"

"Certainly, Doctor," she said. "And after that dreadful trial I'm sure you'll be wanting some roly-polies, too."

The minute she was gone the doctor hustled me into his study. "Listen, Orion," he said. "There might be something I can do for your friends. There are others here who feel as I do about Franklin, and if they're willing to act then perhaps something might be done. But I can't promise you anything, so you mustn't get your hopes up."

He went over to his desk and wrote four notes. He sealed them with wax, then gave them to me along with four silver pennies and told me to go out to the street and hire the first messenger boy who came along. When I got back he was in the hallway, putting his coat and hat on. "I'm going out for a little while," he said. "Don't say a word about any of this to Mrs. Jopson, all right?" Then he left.

A few minutes later Mrs. Jopson came out of the kitchen with a pot of tea and a basket of roly-polies. "Where's the doctor?" she said. "Did he have to run out again? Oh, I do wish people would stop getting sick so the poor man could enjoy his tea for once. Here, dear, have a roly-poly."

I said I didn't want one, and went into the drawing room and sat on the sofa. But I was so fidgety I couldn't sit still. So I put on my coat, and went to the park and tried to walk off my fidgetiness. I stayed outside for about as long as I could stand it, and then I went back to the doctor's house, figuring he must have returned by then. But he hadn't. Mrs. Jopson made dinner for me even though I told her I wasn't hungry. She said she didn't care whether I was hungry or not; I was too skinny, and I needed to fatten up. So I ate just enough to satisfy her, and then I sat down on the stairs and watched the front door. I never knew time to pass so slowly.

At long last, around eleven o'clock, the door opened and in came Dr. Little, shivering and stamping the snow off his boots. I jumped up, all on fire to hear what he'd been up to, but he wouldn't tell me. All I could get him to say was, "The less you know the better," and "Don't worry yourself about it, Orion," and "Go to bed." And when I said I just wanted to help, he said I could—by going to bed! Then he hurried away and shut himself up in his study.

I could see something was up by the hurry he was in, and I figured it wouldn't be too long before it would happen. So I went upstairs and got in bed; but I kept my clothes on and left the door open a crack. Before long I heard Mrs. Jopson clomping up the stairs. Her room was next to mine, and for the longest time I could hear her bumping around in it. I did wish she'd go to bed! At last the bumping stopped. I stared up into the darkness and listened. Everything was still; then through the wall I heard Mrs. Jopson start to snore. A long time went by after that without a peep from downstairs—so long that I began to think I may be wrong about something happening that night. And of course once I got to thinking that, it wasn't long before I decided I *was* wrong.

So I got up, and was about to get out of my clothes when I thought I heard a noise downstairs, like a hinge creaking. I held still and listened. There it is again! In another second I was out of my room and tiptoeing down the stairs; I got to the landing at the bottom just in time to see Dr. Little ease the front door shut behind him. I'd been right after all.

I put on my coat and followed him out. The streets were dark, except for the pools of light under the lampposts, and there were heavy snow flurries coming down. That's good, I thought; it'll make it easier to trail him without being seen. As it turned out I didn't have to worry, because he never once looked back to see if anybody was following him. He made his way to the park, then cut through it and went across the bridge into Cheapside. I followed him down gloomy alleys, and through dark streets, and past tumbledown houses and crumbling old piles of buildings. Everywhere I looked there were shady characters lurking in dark doorways, and drunks brawling in the streets, and men with glowing faces huddled around burning barrels; other men were coming out of pubs, laughing, with ladies on their arms. But no one gave a second look at Dr. Little; it seemed they were used to seeing him at all hours of the night. I hustled along, with my head down, and kept as close to him as I dared.

After a while we came to a dark and deserted part of town filled with grimy factories and run-down old warehouses. Dr. Little slipped around to the back of one of the warehouses and ducked inside through a dark doorway. A minute later I spotted him up on the second floor, going from window to window and pulling the curtains shut.

I was about to go in myself when it hit me that he must be there to meet the people he sent the notes to, and if they hadn't all gotten there yet then one of them might catch me from behind on his way in. So I made up my mind I would hide in the shadows and watch the place for a few minutes to see if anybody else came. Sure enough, before long a man in a dark cloak and one of those funny soup-can hats glided up to the doorway and slipped into the warehouse. Another man came gliding up not long after that and ducked inside. Then here come two more creeping up, one after the other. That's four, I thought; and I was just about to step out of the shadows when here comes a *fifth* man. Who could that be, I wondered? Dr. Little wrote only four notes. The man paused in the doorway and looked around; then he took a cigar out of his pocket and lit it. The glow threw a light onto his face. Peerless! What's that crocodile doing here? The next second he disappeared inside.

I waited another minute to see if anyone else would come along, and when no one did I snuck up to the doorway and slipped though it. It was so dark I had to put out my hands and feel my way along. Pretty soon my foot bumped against the bottom of a staircase. I started up on tiptoe. At the top I came to a door. I eased it open and peeped out onto a large warehouse floor. There were stacks of crates spread around here and there, and from behind one of these stacks came a dim flickering glow and a voice. I crept over to it and peered around the crates. There was Peerless, chewing on his cigar, and the doctor and his friends, all sitting around a candle. I was surprised to see that one of the doctor's friends was Mr. Honey, the clerk from the trial.

Dr. Little was introducing his friends to Peerless. Besides Mr. Honey there was Mr. Brown, who owned the warehouse, and a lawyer called Pilkington, and an old man with shaggy sideburns who looked like a priest; I didn't catch his name.

When he finished with the introductions Dr. Little said, "Thank you for coming, gentlemen. I think it's best if I get straight to the point. Franklin has gone too far this time. We can't stand by and do nothing while those men are—"

"They were found guilty by the jury, Little," said the man with the shaggy sideburns.

"That's because they didn't get a fair trial, Reverend. How could they, with Diggle defending them? That man couldn't find his way out of his own trousers."

"So you want us to petition Franklin for a new trial?"

"You know that would be pointless. Franklin wants them dead so they can't tell the outside world about our colony."

"Then what do you want us to do?"

Dr. Little lowered his voice and said, "Help them escape."

He wouldn't have made a greater stir if he'd pulled a live bearwolf out of his hat. Everyone was flabbergasted—except Peerless—and they all began to speak at the same time. The reverend said, "Why, that's preposterous! It simply can't be done!" Mr. Pilkington said, "I say, old chap. I'm not sure my wife would approve at all." But Mr. Honey, *he* said, "Hold on. Shouldn't we hear him out first?" And Mr. Brown said, "I'm with Honey. We can't say no before we've heard what the good doctor has in mind. Go on, Little."

"Thank you, Brown," said the doctor. "I understand your concerns, gentlemen, but I believe I've come up with a plan that involves minimal risk. Now as we know, the Outsiders are to be taken out to the Valley of Crevasses and left there to die. Without our help, they'll freeze to death in a matter of hours. All I want to do is give them a fighting chance."

"And how do you propose to do that?" said the reverend.

"By hiding a supply of food and equipment near the spot where they're going to be dropped off—just enough to help them make it to Cape Deception and survive until they can be rescued by their own people."

"Poppycock! I still say it can't be done. There are, what—seven of them?"

"Eight. Plus Jones here, and the boy, Orion."

"That's ten. They'd need clothes, tents, medicine, stoves, fuel, sledges, and a hundred other things—not to mention enough food to last until spring. Don't you think Franklin's spies would notice if we tried to gather such a large quantity of food and equipment in one day? And even if they didn't, how would we get it all out to the valley? It can't be done."

"It *can* be done," said the doctor. "Brown can order what we need through his business, and if anybody asks questions he can say he's ordering for his stores. Everything would be delivered here, then tomorrow night after dark we can pack it all into rucksacks and carry it out to the valley. We'd have to make two or three trips, yes, but it can certainly be done. I've already drawn up a list of what we need."

"And what about the bearwolves? How are they supposed to get through miles of bearwolf territory without any guns or ammunition? They wouldn't stand a chance."

"I'm afraid there's nothing we can do about that. I went to the prison this afternoon and spoke to Meriwether about my plan. I told him that we couldn't get any guns, but that didn't bother him. He said they'd take their chances anyway."

"Didn't they bring their own?" said Mr. Brown.

"They brought rifles, yes. But we can't get them, if that's what you're thinking."

"Why not?"

Mr. Honey said, "They're locked up in the evidence room in the courthouse basement. Shanks has the only key."

"Couldn't we steal them?"

"I doubt it. The windows are barred, and the night bailiff padlocks the doors from the inside. He's on duty all night."

"I still say it can't be done," said the reverend.

"My wife would kill me," said Mr. Pilkington.

Dr. Little got mad. "Will we ever stand up to Franklin?" he said. "When he disbanded the Council of Lords, we did nothing. When he sent Lord Blanky down to the mines, we stood by and did nothing. And when Henry Collins begged us to help him escape, what did we do? Why, nothing! If we don't act now, the blood of those men will be on our hands. Now I've put forward a proposal. What do you say?"

The reverend got up. "I say you're mad, Little," he said. "I wash my hands of the whole business." Then he put on his coat and hat and left.

Mr. Pilkington said, "You know my wife, old chap. She'd have my head on a plate if I got mixed up in something like this." And he put on his coat and left, too.

"Oh, pooh!" said Mr. Brown. "Those two would jump at their own shadows. Don't fret, Little. *I'll* help. You just give me that list of yours, and I'll make sure it's all here tomorrow night, ready to pack and take out to the valley."

"Thank you, Brown," said Dr. Little. "And you, Honey?"

"Count me in," said Mr. Honey.

"Good. And you, Jones? Of course we can count on you?"

Peerless flicked his cigar away. He'd been quiet the whole time; a little too quiet, if you ask me.

"Sure, mate," he said with that crocodile smile of his. "You can count on me."

I GET A CRAZY IDEA

THEY talked about the plan for a while longer, and then Dr. Little waited for Peerless and Mr. Honey and Mr. Brown to clear out before he blew out the candle and left. I followed him back to his house and waited in the shadows across the street while he went inside. A few minutes later the light in his bedroom came on. I decided I'd wait until it went out again before I slipped back in, just to be safe.

While I was waiting I got to thinking about the doctor's plan. It seemed like a good one, all in all, except for the part about us not having our rifles. It was true they hadn't done any good in the blizzard, but that was because we couldn't see what we were shooting at. I knew that bearwolves could be killed, because I'd seen one killed in the ice forest. What I didn't know was how we were ever going to get through their territory without our rifles. Then an idea hit me: what if I stole them out of the courthouse myself? Wouldn't Dr. Little be surprised if I turned up at the warehouse tomorrow night with a bunch of rifles! The thought of him patting me on the back and telling me how clever I was swelled my head up so much that I made up my mind I *would* get those rifles, no matter what. The only problem was, how was I going to get into the courthouse? I couldn't see any way.

I noticed that the light in Dr. Little's bedroom had gone out, so I crossed the street and went up to the front door. It was locked! Dang it, why didn't I leave the warehouse early and come back ahead of him? Then I would've been inside the house when he locked the door, not stuck outside in the cold. Wait a minute—that's just the idea I was looking for! Now I knew how I could get into the courthouse.

But I was still locked out of the doctor's house. I tried the drawing room window; it was locked. So I went around the block and slipped down the alley to the back of the house. The kitchen window was locked, too. I climbed up onto the fence and tried to get to one of the windows on the second floor—I mean the first floor—but I couldn't reach the sill.

What am I going to do now, I wondered? Then I noticed the kitchen door. Could it be unlocked? Well, wouldn't you know it, it *was*. Two minutes later I was snug in bed.

When I woke up the next morning it was broad daylight. I lolled around in bed for a while, thinking things over, and then I went downstairs to see about breakfast. Dr. Little had already left the house to go on his rounds, as usual, and Mrs.

Jopson was banging around in the kitchen, as usual.

"Why, look who's finally up," she said. "Here, dear, have a roly-poly to tide yourself over while I make you breakfast."

I took one, and then asked her what time the courthouse closed that day.

"That's an odd question," she said. "Why do you want to know that, dear?"

"I, uh— I was just curious."

"Well, it's an odd thing to be curious about, I have to say. Then again, I suppose children are curious about all sorts of odd things. Did you know that my sister, Mrs. Darlington, has seven of the little dears? Let's see, now. There's Henry, the oldest—he's about your age—and George, and Edward, and William, and Elizabeth, and Anne and Mary. And don't they ask the oddest questions, too! Why, just the other day little Mary asked me if—"

"But do you know?" I cut in.

"Do I know what, dear?"

"What time the courthouse closes!"

"Why should I know that, dear? I've only been there once in my life, and that was yesterday. But if you must know, I suppose it closes at noon, like everything else."

"Noon! But yesterday we were there until after one."

"That's because yesterday was a Thursday, dear. Today is Friday. Everything up here closes early on Fridays."

All of a sudden I was worried.

"What time is it now?" I said.

"Aren't you full of questions! Let's see. It's a quarter to."

"A quarter to *what*?"

"A quarter to noon. Now why don't you sit down and—"

I didn't hear the rest; I was already halfway to the door. I grabbed my coat and knapsack as I ran out of the house, and the next minute I was in the street and making a beeline for the courthouse. I tried to remember how far off it was; about two miles, I thought. I'd have to book to get there by noon.

And I did book; I got there just as Little Ben was starting to clang out twelve. I ran up the steps and pushed my way in through the crowd that was pouring out. There was a desk in the lobby with a big square-jawed bailiff sitting behind it, but there were so many people streaming out that he didn't notice me. The crowd thinned out as I got further in, until at last I turned a corner and found myself in an empty corridor.

I decided I'd better find a place to hide before somebody noticed me, so I opened the first door I came to and peeped inside. It was an office, with a row of desks on one side and a painting of Franklin on the other. I didn't see any place to hide, so I tried the next door down. Another office, just the same. The next door after that opened into a closet that was full of dusty boxes and cobwebs. This'll do, I thought—and I was just about to step into it when a voice called out, "You there, boy! What are you doing?"

My heart jumped, and I turned around. There was a man standing there, looking at me. He had on one of those black gowns and funny powdered wigs they like to wear up there. I didn't recognize him at first, on account of his getup; then I see it's Mr. Pilkington, the lawyer from the warehouse.

"I asked you what you were doing," he says.

"I— I'm looking for my cap, Your Honor," I said. "I left it in the courtroom."

"Oh. Well, you won't find it in there. That's just a broom closet. The courtroom is through those big double doors over there. Here, come with me. I'll help you look for it."

I couldn't exactly say no, and if I ran I'd blow any chance I had of getting the rifles. So I followed him down the hall and into the courtroom, where he helped me look among the pews for my cap—the one I knew was in my knapsack.

After a while he said, "Are you sure you left it in here?"

"Pretty sure," I said.

"Are you sure you were sitting in this section?"

I let on like I was trying to think. Then I said, "Now you mention it, I might've been on the other side. Shoot, I can't remember now. My mind was on the trial."

"Which trial was that?"

"Which trial? It was, uh—my aunt's."

"Who's your aunt?"

"She's, uh—Mrs. Darlington. Mrs. Agnes Darlington."

"Don't know her. What'd she do?"

"She killed my uncle."

"She did! What for?"

"Well, it was her birthday, you see, so she had the whole family over for dinner. I was there, and so were my parents and all my cousins. Let's see. There's Henry—he's about my age—and George, and Edward, and William, and Elizabeth, and Anne, and Mary. Everyone was there except my uncle;

nobody knew where *he* was. Anyway, we're all sitting there, waiting for him, and every minute the food is getting colder and colder, and my aunt, she's getting madder and madder. Well, just when the food's finally good and cold here comes my uncle, roaring drunk. He looks at all of us, then says to my aunt, 'Why, what's all this for, Agnes? It ain't Christmas already, is it?' My aunt didn't say a word, but just got up and left. A minute later she came back in and shot him."

"Shot him! With what?"

Dang it! I'd forgotten that no one in New London except Colonel Gore and his men were allowed to have guns. So I said the first thing that popped into my head.

"A rock."

"She shot him with a rock? How'd she do that?"

"Uh, you know. Like David and What's-His-Name, from the Bible. David and Goliath—that's it."

"Oh! I see. You mean she shot him with a *slingshot*. Well, I suppose I shouldn't be surprised. We humans are good at coming up with creative ways of killing each other."

"*She* didn't kill him—the rock did. That's what her lawyer said, anyway. But the judges didn't buy it."

"Of course they didn't! I'll bet that was Diggle; only he'd use a defense like that. Well, my boy, I'm afraid you'll never see your aunt again. She'll be sent down to the mines, and we all know what happens to people who go there. Hang it! It's a quarter past already. Now *I'm* going to be late, and my wife will kill *me*. Har, har, har! All right. Find your cap and go straight out, understand? The courthouse is closing."

I GET A CRAZY IDEA

After he was gone I shut the doors and looked around for a place to hide. The jury box seemed as good as any, and so I climbed into it and laid down under one of the pews. The floor was cold and hard, so I rolled up my coat and stuck it under my head. I had to wait a good long time before it got dark, after all, and I wanted to be comfortable.

THE THREEPENNY HEIST

I must've drifted off to sleep, because the next thing I knew the courtroom was dark and there was moonlight slanting in through the windows. I stretched, then went over to the doors and put my ear to them; all quiet on the other side.

I remembered Mr. Honey saying that Shanks had the key to the evidence room, so I slipped into the corridor and set off to find his office. Luckily all of the doors had nameplates on them, and it wasn't long before I came across one that said *Silas Q. Shanks, Crown Prosecutor.*

So far, so good, I thought.

I went in. It was your ordinary kind of office, with a row of clerk's desks on one side and a row of file cabinets on the other, and a door at the back that led into a smaller office. This smaller office had a shiny black desk in the middle of it, with nothing on it except for a neat little stack of papers, a pencil with the eraser chewed off, and a black coffee mug that said *Have a Nice Day*. There was a bookcase back there, too, and a coat stand with a lawyer's gown hanging from it. I checked the gown first, thinking that maybe it had a secret pocket, only it didn't. I searched the desk next, but I didn't find any keys in it. Same with the bookcase. So I went back to the outer office and looked through the clerk's desks; no luck there, either. I went through the file cabinets next, one by one; nothing there. Where does he keep the dang thing? Then I happened to notice the coffee mug. Could it be hid under there? I went and looked. Well, there *was* a key under that mug, and it had a tag on it that said *Evidence Room*. I stuck it in my pocket and headed down to the basement.

I found the evidence room easy enough, at the bottom of the stairs, and unlocked the door and went inside. I'd never been in such a creepy room. It had rows and rows of shelves with aisles between them just like you see in any old library, except instead of books on the shelves there were hammers and knives with dried blood on them, and belts and scarves and other things that people had gotten strangled with, and fistfuls of human hair that had been pulled out by the roots and other gruesome things like that. To make it even creepier there was a high window at the back, and the moonlight coming through it gave everything a ghastly blue glow.

I found our rifles on one of the shelves at the back, along with the ammunition. I put the ammo in my knapsack, then slung one rifle over each shoulder and took two in my arms.

I'd planned to take all of them, but I'd forgotten how heavy they were, and four was the most I could carry.

Then something hit me like a bucket of cold water in the face—how am I going to get out? I'd been so satisfied with myself for coming up with a way to get into the courthouse that I never gave any thought to how I'd get out. I couldn't just stroll up to the bailiff and say, "Excuse me, Officer. Will you take the padlock off the doors so I can steal these rifles for my friends who are trying to escape?"

I tried to think of some way to get out, but I couldn't hit on one. I was beginning to worry I might be trapped in there all night when I chanced to look up and notice the window. Of course, I thought—I'll just slide out between the bars.

I found a crate, and stuck it under the window and got up on it. Right away I saw I couldn't get out that way; the bars were too close together. If I'd been Mister Fantastic maybe I could've stretched myself into a noodle and slid out between them, but I wasn't Mister Fantastic. I *wished* I was. The rifles could fit between the bars, but I couldn't.

Wait a minute—the *rifles* can fit. And if I can get the rifles out, then getting past the bailiff would be a piece of cake. So I opened the window—it opened from the bottom and swung in—and then one by one I slid the rifles out through the bars. I squeezed my knapsack out next. Then I took the key back to Shanks's office and put it back under the mug. I headed down to the lobby after that. The big square-jawed bailiff was snoring in his chair, with his chin resting on his chest and his big arms hanging at his side. I gave his sleeve a tug and began to cry. He roused up, looking all startled and alarmed, and said, "Where the devil did you come from?"

"I woke up," I said, "and it was dark, and I didn't know where I was, and there wasn't anybody around, and, and—" Then I busted out crying again.

"There, there," he said, patting me on the head. "There's nothing here to be scared of. You just take a deep breath and tell ol' George everything, from the beginning. Go on, now. It's all right."

So I sniffled, and wiped my nose on my sleeve and said, "I woke up, and—"

"Hold on," he says. "Where'd you wake up?"

"On a pew."

"What pew?"

"I don't know. One of the ones in the courtroom."

"Why, there ain't no pews in the courtroom, son. Pews is in churches. You mean you waked up on a *bench*."

"All right, that's what I mean. A bench."

"What was you doing there? Don't you know the court-house closes at noon?"

"I was at my aunt's trial," I said, "and I fell asleep."

Of course he wanted to know what my aunt did, just like anybody would, so I told him she shot my uncle. Only this time I figured it wouldn't sound like such a stretch if I said she shot him with an arrow instead of a rock. And then I got a little carried away and said that when my dad complained about it she shot *him*, and after that she went berserkers and shot the whole rest of the family—even the kids.

"How come she didn't shoot you?" he said.

"She wanted to," I said, "but she ran out of arrows."

"Ah, that was lucky for you. I tell you, son, I've been night bailiff here going on thirty years, and I've seen every kind of sharp, flimp, lurker, mumper, speeler, and smasher there is come through those doors—and lots of your plain old everyday murderers, too. But I can't recollect a case as strange as your aunt's. Except the Harry Burke case, now I think on it. That was a strange one, I tell you. They say he topped off sixteen people before his wife finally peached on him. Lured 'em home, he did, then got 'em drunk and smothered 'em so he could sell their bodies to some doctor that wanted to dissect 'em. Talk about cheeky! Murdering poor folk so—"

"Can you let me out, Mister?" I cut in. "It's pretty late."

"Oh, yes. I s'pose it is, now I think on it. All right."

So he fished a ring of keys out of his pocket and took the chain off the doors. Then he says, "It must be mighty hard being left to fend for yourself in the cold, cruel world—and you just a boy and all. Now I think on it, I bet you ain't got two pennies to rub together. Here." He dug into his pocket and pulled out three silver pennies. "I'd give you more, but that's all Mrs. Sullivan—that's my wife—lets me have at one time. All right, off you go now. Good luck, son."

I made like I was heading to the street, and when I heard the doors clang shut I doubled back for my knapsack and the rifles. Then I set out for Mr. Brown's warehouse. Even though the streets were quiet I kept to the shadows as best I could; I didn't want anybody to see me with all those rifles.

When I came to the main bridge I hid in the gatehouse and waited until the coast was clear before I scooted across into Cheapside. There were more people in the streets now, so I had to be careful; the last thing I wanted was to get jumped and lose the rifles. But nobody seemed to notice me—or if they did they left me alone, seeing how I was armed to the teeth—and I made it all right to the part of town where the warehouses were. By then the moon had slid behind Mount Terror, and it was so dark all I could see of the warehouses were their outlines, black against the sky.

Well, I was making my way along, trying not to fall into any potholes, when I turned a corner and saw a light ahead. It was coming from one of the warehouses. Somebody must be working late, I thought. But when I got closer I realized the light was coming out of Mr. Brown's warehouse; it was shining out from the second floor for all the world to see.

I was so surprised that I stopped. What's wrong with him, I wondered? Dr. Little isn't stupid. He must know that that light can be seen from a mile away. Why didn't he close the curtains like before? It didn't make any sense.

Then I thought, Maybe something's wrong.

If there was I had to find out, so I slipped around to the back of the warehouse and snuck in. The door at the top of the stairway was open. That's strange, I thought. It isn't like Dr. Little to be so careless; anybody could walk right in on them. I'd better sneak up and see what's going on.

So I started up on tiptoe, trying my best to keep the rifles from knocking together and making any noise. Halfway up

I heard a voice. I froze. I couldn't make out the words, but I recognized the voice easy enough—it was the doctor's. Oh, that's all right, I thought; it's just Dr. Little and his friends. So I started up the stairs again, feeling easier, and pictured how surprised they'd be when I came in with the rifles. But I didn't want to surprise them, so when I got to the top of the stairs I called out, "Dr. Little! It's me!"

The voice stopped; then something heavy fell to the floor with a crash and the light went out, leaving me in the dark. I couldn't understand it. Why'd they put out the light? And what was that crash? Maybe they're just being cautious. Yes, that must be it. They aren't expecting me, after all.

I went the rest of the way up. From the top of the stairs I called out, "It's all right, everybody—it's just me!"

Nobody answered.

That's strange; why doesn't the doctor answer? He knows my voice. I didn't know what else to do, so I began to make my way across the warehouse floor.

All of a sudden—WOOF! WOOF! WOOF!—goes a dog, and an angry voice boomed out, "Uncover the lantern!"

A glare lit up the warehouse—and there was Franklin, and the colonel, and Spartacus, and about a dozen dragoons, all staring at me!

"Seize him!" Franklin roared.

I threw off the rifles and ran. A dragoon made a grab for me and got ahold of my knapsack, but before he could reel me in I twisted out of the straps and got away from him. I ducked under the arm of another one, and was almost back to the stairs and in the clear when Spartacus came bounding up out of nowhere and dragged me down by my sleeve. The next minute Franklin strutted over and hauled me back up to my feet.

"Got you, you little goblin!" he said.

BUSTED!

I glanced around the warehouse. There was the pile of ruck-sacks, all packed up and ready to take out to the valley, and there were Mr. Honey and Mr. Brown, tied up and gagged on one side of it. On the other side Dr. Little was out cold on the floor, with a trickle of blood running down his fore-head; Colonel Gore was standing over him with a billy club in his hand and a stupid grin on his face. As for Spartacus, he just stood there with his tail between his legs, looking a little sorry for what he did to me, and then he slunk off to a corner and flopped down with a sigh.

Franklin ordered Colonel Gore to bind up my hands and search my knapsack. So the colonel got a piece of rope and tied my hands behind my back. Then he emptied my knap-sack onto the floor and began to paw through my stuff.

"Let's see," he says. "One wool cap, red, with a hole in it; one pocket telescope, brass; one pack of superhero trading cards, Special Collector's Edition; one, two, three, four, five, six, seven, *eight* boxes of rifle ammunition; and—let me see here—one, two, *three* roly-polies."

"Confound the roly-polies!" said Franklin. "Do you think I give a straw about roly-polies?" Then he said to me, "Who gave you those rifles and cartridges?"

I clammed up.

"Well?" he said. "Answer me, confound you!"

I clammed up even tighter.

"I'll give you one more chance, you little devil. Well?"

"Go hang!" I said.

Up went his hand, and next I knew I was sprawled out on the floor, with my head ringing like a bell. He let me enjoy the feeling for a minute, and then he grabbed my collar and hauled me back up to my feet.

"Answer me, boy," he said with a growl, "or I'll make you wish you'd never been born."

I believed him; I figured another blow like that would take my head clean off. And since I couldn't see how telling him could make things any worse for Dr. Little and his friends, I decided I may as well keep my head.

"I stole them out of the courthouse," I said.

"That's impossible. Who are you protecting? You'd better tell me the truth this time, or else!" And to show me that he meant business, up went his hand again.

"It's true! Scout's honor."

His hand wavered for a minute; then it came back down. "All right, then," he said. "Prove it. How did you do it?"

I told him. But I wished I hadn't, because then he said to the colonel, "Who's on duty at the courthouse tonight?"

"Tonight?" said the colonel. "Let's see. It's a Friday, so it would be Sullivan, my lord. George Sullivan."

"See that he's arrested at once."

I wanted to kick myself. I never thought I might get anybody in trouble, least of all that nice Mr. Sullivan who gave me his allowance money. I wished I'd let Franklin take my head off. I tried telling him how Mr. Sullivan had nothing to do with it, and how I fooled him into letting me out, but all I got for my trouble was another wallop on the ear.

While my head was still ringing Dr. Little let out a moan and began to stir. The colonel hauled him up by his wrists and plopped him down on a crate. He looked from me to the rifles and then back to me again; he seemed to be having trouble putting it all together. Finally he said, "So that *was* you on the stairs, Orion. How did you get those rifles?"

"Don't pretend you're innocent, Little," said Franklin. "I know you involved this boy in your treasonous plot, and it's a disgrace. He's a mere child."

Dr. Little didn't say anything.

"No matter," said Franklin. "Your fellow conspirators are being rounded up as we speak: Reverend What's-His-Name, and, and— Who's that other one again, Colonel?"

"Pilkington, my lord."

"Pilkington."

"They had nothing to do with this," said Dr. Little.

"Is that right? You mean to tell me that they weren't here with you last night when you hatched your vile scheme? Ah, I see that you don't deny it."

Someone had blown on us, it seemed. But who? Not one of the doctor's friends; Franklin just said they were all being arrested, and you don't arrest your own spies. Peerless? That didn't make any sense, either. Why would he tell on us when he had a chance to escape, too? I was sure he didn't want to spend the rest of his life up there.

Dr. Little didn't say anything, so Franklin got angry and ordered the colonel to take him away. "And those other two traitors, too," he added, waving his hand at Mr. Brown and Mr. Honey.

"To Wormwood, my lord?" said the colonel.

"Yes, of course to Wormwood. Where else, you boob?"

"Certainly, my lord. Anything else?"

"Yes. I'll be accompanying you and your men out to the valley tomorrow with the prisoners. See that my bearwolf is saddled and ready. I mean to take no chances this time."

"I don't quite follow you, my lord."

"I mean the prisoners are to be shot," said Franklin.

"Shot? You mean *shot* shot?"

"Of course that's what I mean! What other kind of *shot* is there? Confound it, Colonel, must I spell out everything for you? They're to be shot, shot, *shot*! That'll teach them not to trifle with John Franklin the Fifth, by Gad. Little and all the other traitors, too. And George What's-His-Name from the courthouse—Sullivan. We'll shoot the whole treasonous lot of 'em. And I hope they all go straight to the devil!"

I felt horrible. Not for myself, I mean—being just a boy and all, I didn't think Franklin would shoot *me* (I was wrong about that, as you'll see)—but for Professor Meriwether and the Sea Leopards, and the doctor and all his friends, and that nice Mr. Sullivan over at the courthouse. It made me sick to think that they'd all be shot in a few hours.

Dr. Little said, "Am I to understand that my friends and I are to be condemned without even the pretense of a trial?"

"You are," said Franklin, as cool as a cucumber.

"I see. And what comes next? Do you intend to proclaim yourself emperor?"

Franklin got so mad it looked like his head might blow off. "Confound it, Colonel Gore!" he said. "Didn't I tell you to take them away? Get them out of here, man!"

The colonel began barking out orders. Two big dragoons took Dr. Little and dragged him off, while others took Mr. Brown and Mr. Honey and dragged *them* off. I wondered if I'd ever see any of them again.

"What about the boy, my lord?" said the colonel.

"Put him under house arrest. I'll decide what to do with him later. He's been a devil of a nuisance ever since he gave us the slip at the lighthouse. And make sure the little fiend doesn't get away from you this time, Colonel."

"Yes, my lord," said the colonel. "Come along, boy."

"Can I have my stuff back?" I said.

"Can the boy have his stuff back, my lord?"

"Oh, bother! I suppose there's no harm in it."

"Including the rifles and ammunition, my lord?"

"Of course not, you boob!"

So Colonel Gore gave me my things, and then he took me by the neck and frog-marched me back to Dr. Little's house. As soon as we got there he sent two dragoons around to the back to guard the kitchen door and rang the doorbell. When Mrs. Jopson answered the door, with her hair in curlers, the colonel shoved me into the house so hard I pitched into her. She threw her big flabby arms around my head, smothering me almost to death, and said to him, "Oh, you horrid man! What have you done to this poor little lamb?"

The colonel just laughed and trotted off, leaving a couple of dragoons to guard the front door. Mrs. Jopson slammed it in their faces.

Of course she wanted to know what I'd done to get myself arrested, and where was the doctor and did I want a roly-poly and about a hundred other things, so while she untied me I told her everything that happened. When I finished she said, "I never did like that man,"—Franklin, she meant—"he has such a dreadful temper. Now listen to me, dear. I haven't the faintest notion whether or not you can help the doctor and your other friends, but I do know this—you must *try*."

"But how?" I said. "Franklin's having them shot at dawn. Besides, I can't even leave the dang house."

"Don't swear, dear. I don't know how you can help them, but you can leave anytime you want."

"How? There's dragoons outside."

"Oh, those are just men with guns, dear; they're as dumb as rocks. I'll show you. But first I have to fix you something to eat. You must be starving, you poor thing."

I *was* starving; I hadn't noticed it until then. So she made me supper, and then after I ate she lit two candles, one for me and one for her, and led me up to the attic. It was full of dusty trunks, and old hatboxes, and busted lampshades and all kinds of other junk. She went over to an old dresser that was pushed up against one wall, and we set our candles on the floor. Then she had me help her shove the dresser out of the way. Behind it was a little door in the wall. She opened it, and then gave me one of the candles and told me to stick my head inside and look. It was a crawlspace, about three feet wide, with a slanting wall on the outside where the roof was and no floor—just the joists.

"This crawlspace connects all the attics on the block," she said. "I used to play in here when I was a little girl. Oh, but that was so long ago!" Then she got all misty-eyed on me.

"I thought this was the doctor's house," I said.

"Oh, no, dear. This house has been in my family since the beginning. The doctor is just a lodger. I took him in after my husband passed—to help make ends meet, you know. Now you mustn't dawdle, dear. Just crawl along until you come to the last door. It will let you into Mrs. Hornby's attic, and then just go down the stairs and out through her kitchen."

"Won't she hear me?"

"Oh, no, dear. She's as deaf as a post." Then she clutched her arms to her bosom, and said, "I do *so* want to hug you before you go, because I know I'll never see you again, you sweet little angel. But I'm afraid you'll set me on fire with that candle. Go on now, dear, and mind the gaps. You don't want to fall through into somebody's bedroom."

I did what she said, and soon I was tiptoeing out of Mrs. Hornby's kitchen into the alley. The moon was still hiding behind Mount Terror, and all I could see of the dragoons guarding the back of the doctor's house—I mean Mrs. Jopson's house—were their cigarettes glowing in the darkness. I crept up the alley and stepped out onto the sidewalk. I had no idea where I was going; I just wanted to get as far away from there as I could, and then I'd find a quiet place somewhere and try to figure something out.

As luck would have it I hadn't even got to the end of the block when here comes Franklin strutting along, with three dragoons. His face turned red when he noticed me, and he thundered, "Stop that boy!"

The dragoons went for me. All three of them were giants, with legs twice as long as mine, and by the time I got over my surprise they'd covered half the distance to me. I didn't wait for them to cover the other half, but spun around and took off like Kid Flash. I hoofed it to the park, and then cut through it, past the mausoleum, and went tearing over the bridge into Cheapside. The next thing I knew I was making my way through a crowd of people who were milling about in front of a pub. Suddenly there was a commotion behind me as the three dragoons charged into the crowd. I heard one of them yell out, "Stop him! Stop that boy!" All the people looked around to see what the matter was; then somebody pointed at me and shouted, "There he is! Thief! Stop him!" Some of the ladies began to scream, and a man in a greasy cap stepped in front of me with his arms out; but I dodged him and went skidding around a corner into another street. This street was dark and deserted. Well, I was racing down the sidewalk, with my lungs on fire, when all of a sudden a pair of hands reached out of an alley and yanked me inside. Someone threw an old coat over my shoulders and pulled a dirty cap onto my head; then someone else pulled me to the ground by my sleeves, and I found myself sitting amongst a little circle of kids. They had sooty faces and were playing a game with a little wooden ball and pins. One of them said, "Look down!" So I looked down.

The next second the dragoons came tearing into the alley. They skidded to a stop; then I heard one of them, all out of breath, say, "The boy that just ran by, where'd he go?"

A voice—a boy's voice—said, "And what boy would that be, your Majesty?"

There was a WHACK!, and the dragoon said, "Play the fool with me again, you grubby little blagger, and I'll thrash the daylights out of you! Now where'd he go?"

"All right, Boss! Keep your hair on. He went thataway."

And off they went again, full tilt, down the alley.

When I couldn't hear their footsteps any longer I got up. A boy with a busted lip was standing there, looking at me. He looked kind of familiar, but I couldn't remember where I might have seen him before. Then I noticed that he had a splint on one of his fingers, and I remembered—he was the boy in Wormwood prison, the one I gave my roly-poly to.

He wiped the blood from his lip, and said, "You're one of them Outsiders, ain't you? What's your name, Guvnuh?"

"Orion," I said.

"Orion, is it? I'm Javelin, but you can call me Jav. This's Shivering Jemmy, and that's Fadge. The little one's Glim."

They all looked about my age, except Glim. He was about six or so, and had curly hair and big ears that stuck out from under his cap. He was the one who told me to look down.

"Right," said Javelin. "We better be off before those three punishers come back."

"Where are we going?" I said.

"To see the king, of course. Where else?"

"King! *What* king?"

"Why, there's only one king around here, Guvnuh—the King of the Flimps!"

THE KING OF THE FLIMPS

I followed them through a tangle of dark, narrow streets and winding alleys till we came to an old pile of a building with busted shutters and a "FOR RENT" sign that looked like it had been there for fifty years. We waited until the coast was clear, then ducked through a hole that was cut in the door and hidden by a flap of canvas. It was pitch-black inside.

Javelin let out a whistle, and in a minute a little voice came out of the darkness and said, "Blam, blam, blam!"

"Flummery and ham!" said Javelin.

It's a password, I thought. And I was right, because then a candle glimmered out of the darkness, and at the top of a rickety staircase I could see a sooty little face with squinty eyes peeping out from behind a door.

"Who's that with you?" said the face.

"Nobody you know," Javelin said.

"Where'd you get him?"

"He fell out of the sky. Is the king in?"

"Yeah. He's showing the new girl some tricks. Come up!"

I followed Javelin up the stairs, with Glim and Fadge and Shivering Jemmy crowding up behind me, and into a room. It had to be the oddest room I'd ever been in. The walls and ceiling were black with soot, and the curtains—if you could call them that, being just strips of newspapers—were held up with forks. On one side there was a glowing fireplace with a bucket of coal next to it, and on the other was a little rug that had a mountain of valuables on it—gold watches, and silver candlestick holders, and pearl necklaces, and walking sticks with handles shaped like dragons' heads, and jewels of every kind. At the back of the room was an old bagged-down sofa with about a dozen kids crowded on it; they were smoking long, thin pipes and watching a boy who was showing a girl how to steal a handkerchief out of his pocket without him knowing she did it. This boy looked about fifteen or so and was as tall and slim as could be. He had on the most splendiferous outfit you ever saw, all bright and showy, with gold cufflinks on the sleeves and silver buckles on his shoes. The girl, I was surprised to see, was the redhead from the trial—the one who got kicked out for calling Shanks a liar.

The boy paid no attention to us, but the girl looked over, and when she saw me she gave a little start. So now the boy looked over, too. He studied me all up and down with his bright green eyes, and said, "Who's the swell, Jav?"

"He's one of them Outsiders," said Javelin.

"Oh, he is, is he? Why'd you bring him here?"

"Some punishers was after him."

"Oh, was they, now? What was they after him for?"

"I dunno, King. They didn't say."

The king asked me why the dragoons were chasing me. I didn't know if I ought to tell him; he might turn me in for a reward. But then I thought, If he wants to turn me in he'll do it whether I tell him or not; besides, he might be willing to help me save my friends. So I decided I'd risk it.

"I escaped out of house arrest," I said.

"You did, did you? Who put you under house arrest?"

"Goggly Eyes—I mean, Franklin."

"The old screw himself? What'd you do to get him mad?"

"I stole some rifles out of the courthouse."

"Did you, now? You hear that, Jav? Our flash friend here nicked some rifles out of the Old Bailey. And why'd you do that, Guvnuh?"

"I was trying to help my friends."

"You was, was you? You still want to help 'em?"

"Of course. I just haven't figured out how yet."

"You hear that, Jav? He hasn't figured out how yet."

"Maybe we should help him," says Javelin.

"Maybe we should," says the king.

"*Can* you help me?" I said.

"Hmm," he said, and he stuck his thumbs in his pockets. "Maybe we can, and maybe we can't. But business first, my flash friend. Right, Jav! What d'ya got?"

"You heard him, boys," said Javelin. "Empty your pockets."

So Glim and Fadge and Shivering Jemmy stepped up and emptied their pockets. Out came silver spoons, and gold cuff links, and shiny cigarette cases, and wallets full of cash, and jingling coin purses. Fadge even pulled a whole cooked ham out from under his coat—and I'd just thought he was fat.

"Nicely done, boys!" cried the king. "Shivering, you and Fadge run them cuff links down to the duffer and tell him I want nine shillings for the lot. Not a penny less, mind you. And don't let him slum you, either, like he done last time."

Shivering Jemmy and Fadge scooped up the cuff links and went out. Then the king says to me, "Now these friends of yours, they're locked up in Wormwood, are they?"

"That's right," I said.

"And at dawn the old screw's going to take 'em all out to the Valley of Crevasses, is he?"

"That's right."

"And then he's going to have 'em all shot, is he?"

"That's— Hey, how'd you know that?"

"I know everything that happens in this town, my friend. You might say it's my business to know."

"So will you help me? There isn't much time."

"I dunno. What d'ya think, Jav? Should we help him?"

"I dunno," says Javelin. "What d'ya think, Glim?"

"I dunno," says Glim. "What d'ya think, Rosie?"

"Of course we should!" said the girl. "We must."

"Hear that, Jav?" said the king. "Rosie says we must."

"Then I thinks we must," said Javelin.

"Me, too," said Glim.

"Hmm," said the king.

I did wish he'd make up his mind! At last he said, "Right. We *will* help you. Do you know why, Guvnuh?"

"No," I said. "Not really."

"It's because one of *your* friends also happens to be one of *our* friends. Dr. Little, I mean."

"Dr. Little's your friend?"

"Let's just say he's done each of us flimps a good turn at one time or another. So is you game?"

"You bet I am!"

He stuck out his long, thin hand, and I shook it. I almost couldn't believe I'd found somebody to help me rescue my friends, but it seemed I had.

"I'm Quicksilver," he said. "And you're Orion—I know already. Right, everybody knows everybody now, so let's get down to business. How long till dawn, Jav?"

Javelin got out his pocket watch and looked at it. "About eight hours, king," he said.

"Right. So we got eight hours to get the doctor and your other friends out of prison and down to the river."

"What river?" I said.

"He wants to know what river, Rosie. Tell him."

"There's a subterranean river that flows from Mount Terror to the sea," said Rosie. "It's called the Acheron. Franklin and his men use it all the time."

"An underground river?" I said. "Really?"

Her eyes flashed. "You don't believe me?"

"No. I mean yes! I mean— I'm just surprised, that's all. If we could've escaped by this river, then why didn't Dr. Little say so? He never said anything about a river."

"That's probably because he didn't think you could escape that way. The entrance is guarded day and night."

"How are we going to get past the guards?"

"We're not. There's another entrance, a secret one that my father found out about. He discovered the original plans for it in the archives and used it to escape. He was going to find help and come back for me, but Franklin hunted him down and had him shot."

She looked like she wanted to scratch someone's face off, and it wasn't hard to guess whose. Then it hit me—her dad was Henry Collins! That's why she looked familiar; she was the little girl in that photo, the one in that silver locket he wore around his neck. Only a few years older, now.

I wanted to know why her dad escaped, so I asked her to tell me about it. She explained how Franklin sent her mom down to the mines for speaking out against him, and how like most people who were sent to the mines she didn't last very long. After that her dad decided to escape. He thought it would be too risky to take Rosie with him, so he stole the map so he could find his way back later and get her out. At first he tried to escape through the Valley of Crevasses, she said, but he was attacked by a bearwolf and would've died if he hadn't been found by a hunting party and brought to Dr. Little. After he recovered he learned about the secret tunnel to the river, and took the *Lady Jane* and got away at last.

When she finished the king said, "Clock's ticking, Orion. We can't get your friends to the river if they're in prison."

"So we have to bust them out," I said.

"Bust 'em out! Ha, ha, ha! That's a good one. The thing is, we can't bust 'em out. Not out of Wormwood. It ain't ever been done, and it can't ever *be* done."

"What are we going to do, then?"

"We're going to get the warden to *give* them to us."

He's crazy, I thought. But when he explained exactly how he was going to get the warden to give them to us, I realized he wasn't crazy at all—he was a genius.

"But first we need a few things," he said.

"What are they?" I said.

"There's five altogether. The first three'll be easy to get— a messenger boy's uniform, some red wax, and a twirl. Glim and the boys can round up them things."

"What's a twirl?"

"It's what you might call a skeleton key."

"All right. What are the other two?"

"Ah, that's where it gets a little tricky. We need Franklin's personal stamp—the one he uses to seal his letters with— and a sample of his handwriting. A letter would be best."

"How are you going to get them?"

"*We* ain't going to get them, my friend," he said. "*You* is."

"Me!" I said. "But how?"

"Steal 'em. How else do you get things?"

"Steal 'em from where?"

"Why, Franklin's house, of course."

BREAKING AND ENTERING

I stared at him.

"You want me to break into Franklin's *house?*" I said.

"You want to save your friends, don't you?" said the king.

"Well, yeah, but—"

"Ain't no buts, Guv. I can't ask any of the boys to do it."

"Why not? Isn't this kind of thing right up their alley?"

"Sure. But this ain't just any house. It's Franklin's. If one of us flimps got caught breaking into it the old screw would ship us to the mines faster'n you can say 'Jack Robinson.'"

"But what if I got caught?"

"Then you won't be no worse off than you is now."

"Yes, I will. I'll be *caught.*"

"You'll be caught anyway, sooner or later. If the old screw wants you bad enough—and I bet he does—he'll turn all of

Cheapside upside down and shake it until you drop out."

He was right, and I knew it. Besides, how could I ask them to do something I wouldn't do myself?

"All right," I said. "Where does he keep the stamp?"

"In his house."

"Where in his house?"

"In his study."

"Where in his study?"

"How should I know? He hasn't invited me over lately."

"Well, can you at least show me where his house is?"

The king looked around. "Right, boys," he said. "Who's up for showing Orion here the way to Franklin's house?"

No one said anything.

"Come on, boys. You don't have to go inside."

Dead silence.

So then Rosie said, "Fine. *I'll* show him. I'm not afraid of Franklin."

"All right, let's go," I said, and I started for the door.

"Oy!" said the king. "Not looking like that you don't. All of Cheapside will be crawling with punishers by now; you'll stand out like a sore thumb. Look at yourself—swanky new shoes, posh coat, hardly no dirt on your face. You won't get to the end of the block looking like that. Wad'ya think, Jav? Should we turn Orion here into a proper flimp?"

"I dunno," says Javelin. "Should we, Glim?"

"I dunno," says Glim. "Should we, Rosie?"

"Of course!" says Rosie.

"Hmm," says the king. "Then I thinks we *will*. Spithead!"

One of the flimps hauled himself off the sofa and rolled up to us in a cloud of dust. There was so much grime caked on his face the only part of it you could see was his eyeballs, and his clothes were like—well, maybe I won't tell you what his clothes were like, because you probably wouldn't believe me anyway. As for the smell he gave off, it wouldn't be much of a stretch to say it would have stopped a charging bearwolf. The king had me swap clothes with him, then he got the coal bucket and smeared some coal dust on my face. After that he stepped back and looked me over.

"Well, Jav? Do he look like a right proper flimp or what?"

"That he do," said Javelin. "A right proper flimp."

"Right. *Now* you two can shove off. And if I don't see you again, 'twas nice making your acquaintance."

I started for the door, but Rosie didn't budge. "What's the matter now?" I said. "The king said we could shove off."

"Do you have a knife?" she said.

"Yeah, I got a pocketknife. Why?"

"Cut off a piece of that ham."

"You're hungry *now*? Can't you wait till we get back?"

Her eyes flashed. "Franklin has a dog, remember?"

Spartacus! I'd forgotten about him. And that was just the kind of thing that could get us caught, too.

I sawed off a piece of ham and put it in my pocket, then we left for Franklin's house. When we got outside the street was dark, and there wasn't a soul in sight. All the pubs and bawdy houses were dark, too.

"Where is everybody?" I said.

"I don't know," said Rosie. "Something's not right. The pubs are usually open all night."

"We'd better be careful. Lead on."

We set off again, with Rosie leading. We hadn't gone far when we came around a corner and ran into a little clump of ladies walking arm-in-arm the other way. They stopped, looking surprised, and stared at us. We stared back at them. There were three of them, all young and pretty, with bright red lips and high heels showing under their long coats.

"Pardon us!" said Rosie.

"Oh, no," said the one in the middle. "Pardon *us.*"

Nobody said anything. Then Rosie said, "My, the streets are quiet tonight."

"You ain't heard yet, missy?" said the same lady. "They've put a curfew on Cheapside. Me and me girlfriends was just heading home. You and your friend better head home, too, before the punishers catch you out of doors."

"Oh! We didn't know. What's it about?"

"Lordy, they never tell us nuthin', do they? But the word is that one of them Outsiders escaped from house arrest. A whole company of punishers chased him into Cheapside— more than forty, some folks say—and all of 'em big, strong, strappin' men. But he gave them the slip, so his lardship put Cheapside under curfew. There's punishers going house to house, kicking in doors and causing all sorts o' trouble."

"How dreadful! Is he dangerous?"

"Oh, no, missy. I don't see how he could be. They say he's only a boy, about eleven or so, and tall for his age. Just like your friend here"—she looked at me—"only he's dressed like a lil' gen'lman, in a fine black coat and shiny new shoes."

Rosie thanked her and said we'd head right home. As soon as we got around the next corner she stopped me, and said, "If there's a curfew all the bridges will be closed. Franklin's house is on the other side of the chasm."

"We have to get across," I said. "Will there be guards?"

"Let's go see. We'd better keep out of sight."

So we kept to the shadows, and made no more noise than ghosts. It was a good thing we did, too, because before long we started seeing squads of dragoons marching double time up and down the streets and running in and out of buildings. From inside the buildings we heard doors being kicked in, and things getting smashed, and ladies screaming and babies crying. It seemed Franklin wanted to find me pretty bad.

At last we turned a corner and spotted a bridge up ahead. Sure enough, there were two dragoons standing guard near the gatehouse. One looked around sixty, the other thirty or so; and both had clubs. They were dropping pebbles off the side of the bridge and watching them fall into the chasm.

We tried to think of a way to get by them, but neither of us could come up with anything. Then I happened to shove my hands into my pockets—to warm them up, you know, it being as cold as Christmas—and one of them brushed up against the ham. That gave me just the idea we needed.

"I got an idea," I said. "Come on."

I stepped out from the shadows and started for the bridge, trying to look all calm and casual even though my heart was going a hundred miles an hour. Rosie came with me. When the dragoons noticed us they dropped all their pebbles and whipped out their clubs. My legs suddenly felt like jelly.

"Hold it right there!" said the older dragoon, holding up his hand. "Just where do you two think you're going? Don't you know there's a curfew in place?"

"It's all right, officers," I said. "We're on official business."

"Oh, is that so? And what business might that be?"

"Courthouse business. Mr. Sullivan, he forgot his supper again, so Mrs. Sullivan hired us to bring it to him." I hoped they hadn't heard that he'd been arrested.

"Sullivan? I don't know nobody named Sullivan."

"You know— *George* Sullivan. Works at the courthouse."

"Don't know him."

"Hold on," said the younger dragoon. "Do you mean the George Sullivan that's night bailiff there?"

"That's the one," I said.

"Why, I know him! He's married to my aunt's gardener's hairdresser. So you two know ol' George, do you?"

"Sure do. We bring him his supper all the time."

"All right, then. You can go on across."

"Not so fast, Henry," said the older one. He narrowed his eyes at me and said, "What's this fellow look like?"

"Well," I said, "he's pretty gigantic, and he's got a square kind of face with a square kind of jaw. It makes him look a little mean, but he's really as nice as could be."

Henry laughed. "That's George to a 'tee.' All right, go on across. And tell him Henry Sims said hello."

"Not so bloody fast, Henry!" said the older dragoon. "Do you always have to be jumping the gun?" Then he looked at me and said, "Let me see this supper you say you have."

I showed them the piece of ham. Henry looked satisfied, but the older dragoon didn't; not by a long shot. "Why, that ham's got crud all over it," he said. "It ain't fit for a dog."

"Oh, George won't mind," I said. "He ain't particular."

"How much did Mrs. Sullivan pay you to deliver it?"

"How much? It was, uh—three pennies."

"Let me see 'em."

I showed him the three silver pennies that Mr. Sullivan had given me. And would you believe it? He *still* wasn't satisfied. Then Henry jumped in, thank goodness, and said, "Hang it, John. Can't you see that this ain't the boy we're lookin' for? He don't fit the description at all. Why don't you just let the little gamins bring George his supper?"

"Oh, all right," said John. "But hurry back!"

We crossed the bridge and made like we were heading to the courthouse; then once we were out of sight we doubled back around and headed west. Pretty soon the houses began to get bigger and grander. They weren't all jammed together like Mrs. Jopson's, either, but stood off by themselves behind walls and gates. Finally we came to the biggest and grandest house of them all. It had a wall running all the way around it and an iron gate with a big padlock on it. This house had four floors, and as many as forty-seven chimneys, and more windows than you could count. They were all shuttered, but in some of them you could see light leaking out through the chinks in the shutters; and sometimes the light would flicker, and we knew that somebody was walking around in there.

We climbed a tree that was growing close to the wall and dropped down on the other side. Then we slipped around to the back of the house, keeping out of the moonlight as best we could, and began to look for a way in. We checked every window that didn't have any light coming from behind it, but they were all locked. The doors were locked, too. I whispered to Rosie and said we'd have to find a rock and smash one of the windows. But she said no, somebody might hear us, and we should only do it as a last resort. First we should go back and check again, in case we missed something.

So we crept along the back of the house again. We heard noises coming from many of the rooms, so I whispered to Rosie and said that Franklin must have an awful big family to fill such a big house. Rosie whispered back and said he didn't have any family at all; it was only him and his wife, Lady Franklin. All the rest were servants.

Well, that got me thinking about all the servants I'd have to sneak past to get to the study, and I didn't watch where I was going and barked my shin on something. It hurt so bad I opened my mouth to let out a yell; but Rosie clamped her hand over it, and saved us.

When we looked down to see what I'd barked my shin on we saw a little iron door built into the side of the house. It said COAL on it. I gave the handle a tug and the door swung open. We got on our knees, and when we peered inside we saw a narrow chute slanting down into the dark.

"Wait for me here, all right?" I said.

And then I squeezed through the opening and slid down headfirst into the darkness.

WHAT I HEARD IN THE STUDY

DOWN I went, faster and faster; and then—WHOOOSH!—I plowed into something that spread out from under me with a noise like little rocks rolling down a hill, and some kind of dust rose up and got in my eyes and throat. It was so dark I couldn't see what I'd slid into, and I couldn't imagine what it could possibly be. Then I remembered what it said on the little iron door. Of course, I thought—I'm on a pile of coal.

I got up and spit the soot out of my mouth. Then I began to make my way through the darkness, nice and easy, with my hands out in front of me. Before long I ran up against a wall. At this rate I could be wandering around down here till doomsday, I thought. Why didn't I think to bring a light?

All of a sudden I heard footsteps over my head; then keys jangling. Somebody's coming! Before I could budge a door opened and light came flooding down a set of stairs; luckily I happened to be standing underneath them, or I would've been seen. I crouched down in the shadows as a stiff-necked man in a butler's uniform came gliding down the stairs. He glided over to a rack that was filled with dusty old bottles of wine and began to rummage through them.

I was in a real jam now. If I waited for him to go I would only be locked in the cellar again, but if I tried to sneak up the stairs behind his back he might turn around and see me.

What should I do?

I decided I had to risk it. So I slid out from the shadows and started up the stairs on tiptoe, with my heart going like a jackhammer. At any minute I expected to hear a voice bark out, "You there, stop!", or see a maid appear in the doorway at the top of the staircase, with a feather duster, and let out a scream. But neither of those things happened, thankfully, and I made it to the top of the stairs all right.

I peeped out into a long hallway. It was lit up as bright as heaven, it seemed to me, and had more doors than I could count. I started down it. I heard voices coming from behind some of the doors, and glasses clinking and other noises like that. I felt a little weak, but I forced myself to keep going. I peeked behind the first door I came to that didn't have any light leaking from under it and saw a room like the drawing room in Mrs. Jopson's house, only about ten times grander. Anyway, it wasn't the study, so I kept going. A little further down I came to a mirror, and when I saw myself in it I was so surprised that all I could do was gawk. I was black from head to toe; perfectly black, like I'd been dipped in a barrel of tar. Even my teeth were black.

Suddenly I heard a noise, and when I looked back up the hallway there was the butler, with a bottle of wine, closing the cellar door! I slipped through the nearest door and eased it shut; then I put my ear to the crack.

Footsteps, coming this way!

At the same time there was a growl behind me.

I turned around, ever so slow—and there was Spartacus, flopped down in front of a fireplace, with his ears standing up. He let out another growl. I pulled the piece of ham out of my pocket and tossed it over to him. He looked at it for a minute; then at me; then at the ham again. I did wish he'd make up his mind! Finally he snapped it up in his big jaws, and down the hatch it went. Then he settled his head back down on his paws and heaved out a sigh.

By this time the footsteps had almost reached the door, so I looked for a place to hide. There was a desk in front of the fireplace and bookcases along all the walls except one, where there was a window with drapes over it. I ran over to it, and just as I jumped behind the drapes the door opened and in comes the butler with his bottle of wine. He glided over to the desk, where he poured some wine into a glass that was sitting on a little silver tray, and then he went back to the door and stood at attention. What's he doing, I wondered?

I didn't have to wonder long, because pretty soon in struts Franklin himself, looking angry and annoyed. He went over to the desk and pulled out his pocket watch.

"Confound it!" he muttered to himself. "It's already after midnight, and I still have to write that blasted letter."

"Will that be all, m'lord?" said the butler.

"I'll be going up to bed soon. Is my room ready?"

"Yes, m'lord. However—"

"However what? Spit it out, man. I have work to do."

"It's— It's your fireplace, m'lord. I'm afraid it's not lit."

"Confound it, Andrews! My room will be an icebox."

"I'm terribly sorry, m'lord. Your fireplace began to smoke when I tried to light the fire, so I had to send for a chimney sweep. He should be here soon."

Franklin confounded him again and sent him away. Then he took out a sheet of paper and wrote his letter. When he was finished he reached under his desk and fiddled around with something. There was a little CLICK!, and a panel on the side of the desk popped open. I'll be danged, I thought; it's a secret compartment—and inside was the dispatch box. Franklin unlocked it and took something out of it; it was his personal stamp. There were some letters in there, too.

Just then there was a knock at the door.

"What is it now?" said Franklin.

Andrews glided in. "Colonel Gore to see you, m'lord," he said. "And he has a—a gentleman with him."

"It's about time. Show them in."

Andrews left, and in a minute the colonel trotted in with the last person I expected to see there—Peerless.

"What's this about, Franklin?" he said. "It's the middle of the bloody night! I was asleep."

"Mind your tone with His Lordship," said the colonel.

"I'll speak as I please, dogface. If you don't like it you can go dance with the ding—"

Colonel Gore whipped out his club and doubled Peerless over with a blow to his stomach. I'd never seen anything like it; it was so savage it took my breath clean away from me.

Franklin laughed and said, "Stand him up, Colonel." The colonel stood Peerless up. "Do you recall what we discussed before the trial, Mr. Jones?" said Franklin.

"Yeah," said Peerless, with an eye on Colonel Gore. "You wanted me to lie at the trial and spy on that doctor bloke. I agreed to do it for a hundred thousand gold sovereigns and safe passage off this godforsaken rock."

So it *was* Peerless who blew on us. I should've known it all along; it was just the kind of crocodilish thing he *would* do. Now I understood why he lied at the trial, too.

"Do you also recall my answer?" said Franklin.

"Yeah," said Peerless. "You said you'd take care of me."

"Yes, I did. And I intend to do just that—*take care of you*. I've decided that you'll be rejoining your comrades. I think the colonel has already informed you of their fate."

Peerless turned white. "You mean I'm to be shot?"

"If you want to put it like that, yes."

"How else would I put it!"

Franklin shuffled his papers. He looked bored.

"Crikey, Franklin!" said Peerless. "You can't be serious."

"You are gravely mistaken if you think that."

"But why?"

"Why? Because if I allowed you to leave this island, you'd tell the world about our little colony. I can't allow that."

"I promised I'd keep my mouth shut, didn't I?"

"You must take me for a fool, Jones, if you think I'd trust the word of a man who so easily betrays his own comrades. Get him out of my sight, Colonel."

"Wait! Listen, Franklin. I swear on my mother's—"

Colonel Gore shut him up with another blow, and then a couple of dragoons came in and dragged him away, kicking and screaming. When it was quiet again Franklin asked the colonel if I'd been found.

"Not yet, my lord," said the colonel. "But he will be."

"Don't underestimate him, Colonel. He's smarter than he looks."

I didn't know if that was a compliment or an insult. The colonel said, "With all respect, my lord, he's just a boy."

"Just a boy! Confound it, Colonel, that boy is the reason the Outsiders came here in the first place. He kept the map from us at the lighthouse, didn't he? And he stole those rifles right out from under our noses. He might be just a boy, but he's been a confounded nuisance from the beginning. I wish the little devil were here right now. I'd wring his neck!"

I didn't wish I was there.

After Franklin calmed down he sealed the letter with his stamp and gave it to the colonel with orders to take it to the warden without delay. The colonel snapped out a salute and trotted off. Franklin put the dispatch box away, and then he drained his glass of wine and left.

The minute he was gone I slipped out from behind the drapes and shut the door. Now for the stamp! I went over to the desk and looked for the button, or switch, or whatever it was that opened the secret compartment. I found it easily enough, and got out the dispatch box and put it in my coat pocket. Then I went back over to the window, thinking I'd slip out of the house that way, but the dang latch was rusted shut and I couldn't budge it. I'll just have to go out the way I came in, I thought. So I opened the door and peeped into the hallway; all clear. In no time I was at the cellar door.

It was locked!

For the second time that night I felt sick; I never thought I might get locked *out* of the cellar. And now there I was, in a house full of servants, with Franklin's dispatch box poking out of my pocket and no idea how to get out without being seen. If that wasn't bad enough, I was black from head to toe with coal dust. Could it get any worse?

All of a sudden I heard an awful shriek, followed by the most outrageous clanging and clattering; they must've heard it in China. I turned around, with my heart in my mouth, and there was a maid standing there, gawking at me, with her hands clapped over her mouth and a platter lying at her feet. About a hundred pieces of silverware used to be on it, but now they were scattered all over the floor. She couldn't have found a way to make more noise if she'd wanted to.

Doors started flying open up and down the hallway, and before I knew it I was surrounded by about twenty servants, with the ones in front gaping at me, the ones further back stretching their necks to get a better look at me, and all of them asking what it was about. I couldn't have gotten away if I'd wanted to; they had me hemmed in. The next minute here comes Andrews pushing through the crowd. When he spotted me he looked as sour as grapes, and took me by the ear and marched me off to the kitchen.

"Just what do you think you're doing here?" he said when we got there.

I opened my mouth, but nothing wanted to come out.

"Oh, never mind," he said. "Did you finish?"

"Finish?" I said.

"Yes, finish! Are your ears full of soot, too? Did you finish sweeping out the chimney in His Lordship's bedroom?"

"Oh! That. Yup, it's as clean as a whistle."

"Good. Out you go, then. If His Lordship found you in this section of the house there'd be a devil of a price to pay. And do you know who'd pay it? I would."

He marched me over to the kitchen door, and was about to shove me out when he stopped and asked me if anybody had paid me yet. I said no. So he took out a little purse and gave me ten silver pennies. Then he shoved me out.

The minute I got out of his sight I cut over and doubled around to the back of the house. And when I got to the coal door there was Rosie, waiting for me.

MY INTERVIEW
WITH THE WARDEN

OF course she wanted to know everything, so on our way back to Cheapside I filled her in. Then I showed her the ten silver pennies. She couldn't believe it. I couldn't, either.

We got back across the bridge and to the flimps' hideout without any trouble, and then ducked in through the hole in the door. Rosie let out a whistle.

No answer.

She whistled again, a little louder.

Still no answer.

"Something's wrong," she said.

"Let's go see," I said.

We went up the stairs on tiptoe, and eased the door open and looked into the room. It was empty. No flimps, no loot, no sofa, no coal bucket; even the fireplace was cold and dark. I couldn't understand it. Where'd they all go?

Then suddenly a little voice came out of the darkness and said, "Blam, blam, blam!"

Rosie gave the password. A candle shone out from behind a panel in the wall on the other side of the room, and in the light of it we could see a little head with curly hair and big ears. It was Glim.

"What're ya waitin' for?" he said. "Get in!"

We scooted across the room and climbed through a little hole in the wall. Glim shut the panel behind us, and then led us down a passage and up a staircase. At the top we came to an attic that was all a-glow with candles. And there was the old sofa with all the flimps crowded together on it, and the rug with the loot, and the coal bucket. The king was sitting at a table, sorting a big pile of coins—pennies, and shillings, and farthings, and sovereigns, and crowns, and half crowns and all the other funny coins they have up there—into neat little stacks. He looked surprised when we came in. "So you wasn't caught?" he said. "I thought maybe you was."

"What's everyone doing in here?" I said.

"Hiding. After you left we got word punishers was going house-to-house hunting for you, so I had the boys shift the swag in here. We wouldn't want to get caught with it now, would we? So did you get the goods?"

I set the dispatch box on the table.

"Good on you! Didn't I say they'd pull it off, Jav, if they wasn't caught first?"

"That you did, King," said Javelin. "That you did."

"Right. Let's get down to business. Where's Cracker?"

A boy with sharp little eyes got up off the sofa and came strolling over, cracking his knuckles. He took a wallet with a set of lock-picking tools in it out of his pocket, and in two seconds flat he had the dispatch box open.

"Right," said the king. "Now for Tricky Dick."

Another boy, with inky fingers, strolled over and took the king's place at the table. He took a sheet of paper out of one pocket and a little bottle of ink and one of those pens made from a goose feather out of another. Then he pulled one of Franklin's letters out of the dispatch box and studied it.

"Tricky's the best forger in New London," said the king. "When he's done with our letter, not even Franklin himself will be able to tell it from one of his own."

Then he started talking, and Tricky began writing. When the letter was finished the king looked it over and claimed it was the best letter he ever wrote. (Later on I found out that he couldn't read; none of the flimps could, except for Rosie and Tricky.) Anyway, this is what the letter said:

> *To the Warden of Wormwood Prisen:*
> *You is hearby ordered to deliver Perfesser Merry-*
> *wether, Docter Litle, and the rest of that pesky lot*
> *(not fergetting big Jorge Sullavan, that was night*
> *bayliff there at the courthouse), to Kernel Goar in*
> *Lower Slag Lane at dawn. Don't deliver them to*

wherever it was I ordered you to deliver them to before. I changed my mind about that, so do the other thing instead. Oh, and from now on I want you to serve figgy-dowdy to the prisoners twice a day, instead of that slumgullion you call stew.

By Order of His Lardship,

The Honerable John Franklen, Fifth

"Well?" said the king. "What d'ya think?"

I said I thought the letter was top notch, and I couldn't see how it wouldn't fool the warden. But when Rosie saw it she looked horrified. "We can't use this!" she said.

"Why not?" said the king.

"Because it's— Well, it has a few mistakes in it, that's all. The warden might notice. We should do it over."

The king said all right, so with Rosie's help Tricky started on a new letter. But before they got even halfway through it he ran out of ink. He didn't have any more, so we had to go with the first letter; nobody could see any other way. Tricky folded it, then melted a little puddle of red wax on the flap and pressed Franklin's stamp into it. Meanwhile I scrubbed the coal dust off my face and neck and hands, and got into the messenger boy's uniform they had stolen for me. When I was ready to go I stuck the letter in my pocket and set out for the prison. I went by myself this time, and didn't try to stay out of sight; I didn't have to, because whenever a squad of dragoons stopped me I would just whip out the letter, and when they saw Franklin's stamp on it they'd stiffen up like statues and stand at attention until I was out of sight.

At the prison the guard led me to the warden's office and told me to wait there while he went and fetched him. After a few minutes here comes the old vampire himself, rubbing his eyes and wearing a sleeping cap and a grubby nightshirt that hung down to his bony knees.

"What is it this time?" he grumbled. "Can't a man sleep?"

I held out the letter and said, "Got a letter for you."

He squinted at me. "Take off your cap," he said.

I took off my cap.

"Don't I know you?" he said.

"Don't believe so."

"Yes, I do! You were here the other day with that irksome doctor. What're you doing in a messenger boy's uniform?"

"I'm a messenger boy."

"Since when?"

"Since I got a job as one."

"Who gave you a job as one?"

"Who? It was, uh—Franklin."

"His Lordship gave you a job? That don't sound like him."

"Well, he did."

"Why?"

"Because I asked him for one. I have to eat, don't I?"

"Hmm," he said. "I think you're lying."

I could see I had to resort to more drastical measures; so I dropped my chin, and sniffled, and said I *wasn't* lying, and it was the hardest kind of work being a messenger boy because they took half my wages to pay for the uniform and most of the rest for taxes, and no one ever tipped, and everything up there cost an arm and a leg, and—and— Then I broke down and dropped tears all over my shoes.

The warden screwed up his face, and said, "Oh, stop that infernal blubbering! Do you think I care about your troubles? Here, give me that letter." He snatched it out of my hand. "Why, this is from His Lordship! Why didn't you say so?"

Before I could say, "Because you never gave me a chance, you crusty old boob," he broke the seal and began to read the letter. And the longer he read, the more puzzled he looked. "This is odd," he said at last. "Very odd."

He went and got a strongbox out of his desk, and took a letter out of it. I bet that's the letter Franklin wrote when I was in his study, I thought. Well, it was. The warden set the two letters side by side and began to study them. Finally he scratched his chin and said, "I'll warrant the handwriting is His Lordship's, but I'll be boiled in haggis if he wrote this letter you brought me. His spelling is impeccable, for one thing, and the orders in it contradict the ones Colonel Gore brought me less than an hour ago."

Then he glared at me.

Crying won't get me out of this, I thought; I better come up with something quick. So I groped around for an idea— and right away I hit on one.

"That's because he was jingled when he wrote it," I said.

"He was what?" said the warden.

"Jingled. You know—drunk."

"His Lordship drunk? I don't believe it."

"Ask Andrews. He was there when His Lordship did it."

"Did what?"

"Drank a whole bottle of wine—in one go."

"His Lordship drank a whole bottle of wine in one go?"

"Yup."

He came and stood before me, with his bony hands on his hips; then he bent down until his nose almost touched mine. I tried to swallow, but I couldn't; my mouth was too dry.

"You're lying," he said.

"Whatever," I said.

He looked puzzled. "What does that mean?"

"It means if you don't believe me, why don't you write to Lord Franklin and ask him yourself?"

"Fine," he said. "I will." And he went back to his desk and pulled out a piece of paper and a goose feather pen.

"Fine," I said. "Go ahead. I'll bring back his answer."

"Fine," he said. And he started writing.

"Of course," I said, "I'll have to wake him up."

He stopped writing.

"Wake him up?"

"Well, sure. It's the middle of the night, ain't it? He'll be asleep. And when he wants to know why I had him woken up in the middle of the night, I'll have to tell him that the warden didn't believe that his letter was real—even though it had his *personal stamp* on it. You know what he'll say?"

"What?"

"He'll say, 'Confound the warden! Who does he think he is, waking me up in the middle of the night with this nonsense? You march straight back there and tell that crusty old boob that if he doesn't follow my orders, I'll ship him off to the mines faster than you can say 'Jack Robinson.' Confound him!' *That's* what he'll say. I can hear it now."

The warden put down his pen; his hand was trembling. He licked his lips, and said, "On second thought, perhaps it would be better not to disturb His Lordship. It's really just a matter of a few misspelled words, after all. I'd be obliged to you if we could keep this little matter between ourselves, young man. Here, this is for you."

He took a gold sovereign out of the strongbox and gave it to me; then he called the guard in and ordered him to show me out. When I got back to the flimps' hideout everybody wanted to know how it went, so I told them all about my interview with the warden and then showed them the gold sovereign. The king was as pleased as he could be.

"You look pretty knackered, Orion," he said. "Why don't you get in a few winks? Rosie'll wake you up when it's time to go. Oy, you lot! Clear off the sofa."

I was pretty tired, come to think of it. So after I got back into my own clothes I laid down on the sofa and closed my eyes. Before I knew it I was asleep.

WHAT HAPPENED IN
LOWER SLAG LANE

IT seemed like I'd just closed my eyes when there was Rosie, shaking my shoulder and saying it was time to go. The king and Javelin and the rest of the flimps had gone ahead to get everything ready, so we grabbed our coats and my knapsack and headed out. There were lights on in some of the houses now, and in the stores we could see the shopkeepers getting ready to open for the day. We reached Lower Slag Lane just as the sky was beginning to lighten up in the east. I'd never seen a rougher street, with seedy pubs and flophouses all up and down both sides, and everywhere the roughest kinds of people. There were sour-mouthed old ladies in shabby coats sweeping the sidewalks, and men with sweaty faces unloading barrels from vans, and other men stumbling out of pubs, wiping their mouths on their arms and looking for trouble. The king couldn't have picked a better spot.

Halfway down the lane we turned into an alley that was so narrow we had to enter it single file. When we got in a little ways we found the king, and Shivering Jemmy, and Fadge and Glim waiting for us in the shadows. The king was just beaming. He took a key out of his pocket and gave it to me. "Here's the twirl," he said. "Remember what to do with it?"

"Yeah," I said. "First unlock the door, then the shackles."

"Right. And where do you go after you got 'em sprung?"

"Down the alley, over the bridge, into the mausoleum."

"Right. We'll all be waiting for you there. Oy! It's almost dawn. Everybody get in your places."

Everybody got in their places—Glim in front, nearest the lane; Shivering Jemmy and Fadge behind him; then Rosie; then me; and last the king. By this time we could see a pink glow spreading up over the sky. It got brighter and brighter, until finally a ray of sunshine fell across the building on the other side of the lane. The king tapped me on the shoulder and said the van should be along any minute now. I hoped he was right; I was so jittery I thought I might burst.

Five minutes dragged by, and still no van.

I began to wonder if something had gone wrong. The king looked worried, too. I was about to ask him if he would send somebody to find out what was going on, when here comes Javelin running into the alley with his face all a-glow.

"They're coming!" he said. "They had a flat was all."

"Right!" said the king. "Get back out there!"

Javelin ran back out to the sidewalk; then he leaned against a lamppost, trying to look cool and casual, and watched the lane. Pretty soon we made out the CHUG! CHUG! CHUG! of a steam engine. It got louder by the second.

All of a sudden Javelin's hand flew up to his ear.

"That's the signal!" said the king. "Go, Glim!"

Glim shot out of the alley like a monkey out of a box and ran into the street. Javelin waited for him to go by, then let out a whoop and took off after him; so did Shivering Jemmy and Fadge. "Get him, boys!" Javelin sang out. Everybody in the lane stopped what they were doing and looked around to see what all the hoopla was about. Then I heard someone cry, "Watch out, child!"; there was a screech of brakes and a sickening kind of THUD!, and next I see Glim flying through the air and landing in a heap on the cobblestones. I'd never seen anything done so well.

I could see the prison van now, big and gray and hulking, stopped just outside the alley. People were running toward it from every direction, while other people were spilling out of pubs and flophouses, some of them still buttoning up their coats. As for Glim, he was curled up in the lane with blood all over his face—or that's what it looked like, anyway.

"Now, Rosie!" said the king.

Rosie ran out of the alley. She pushed through the crowd to where Glim was all curled up and cried out, "Oh, Oliver! Oliver!" Then she rained tears all over the place.

Meantime the driver had climbed down out of the van and was making his way through the crowd. He was a big, ugly, mean-looking man in a bailiff's uniform, and he had a club. "Let me through!" he growled. "Let me through, I said!"

If he'd known what was good for him he would've stayed in the van. When he reached the middle of the crowd Rosie whirled on him and said, "You killed my baby brother!"

"Rubbish," he said. "I didn't kill nobody. The little rat ran right in front of my van. Anyhow, he ain't dead. Can't you see he's still breathing? He'll be as good as new in five or six months." Then he said to a man in a green cap, "You there! Drag this little urchin out of my way. I'm in a hurry."

"What d'ya mean, drag him out of your way?" said the man in the green cap. "Can't you see he's hurt?"

"Oh, blazes!" said the driver. "I'll do it myself."

"Don't you touch him, you brute!" said Rosie.

She stepped in front of him with her arms out, but he just swung his arm—the one with the club in it—and brushed her aside. He didn't actually *strike* her with the club, but it must've looked like he did, because a gasp went up from the crowd, and a lady with a shawl cried out, "Merciful heaven! He just clubbed that poor girl! Joe Geater, don't just stand there with your mouth hanging open—do something!"

The man with the green cap made a grab for the club. He got hold of it, but the driver yanked it out of his hand and knocked him out with a single blow. The lady in the shawl let out a shriek and said, "Joe! Oh, now he's gone and killed my husband!"

And without any further ado she leaped onto the driver's back and started clawing up his face. There was another big bailiff in the van who'd just been sitting there up until then, watching the show; now he jumped down and charged in to help his friend. He had a club, too, and he wasn't shy about using it on the lady with the shawl. That didn't sit well with the other ladies in the crowd, so *they* charged in to help *their* friend—and most of the men did, too—and the next thing you knew the two bailiffs had their hands full.

"It's show time, Orion!" said the king. "Good luck!"

I took off and sped out of the alley. By that time it was a full-scale brawl between the two bailiffs, with their clubs, and the people of Lower Slag Lane, with their fists and feet and fingernails. I would've liked to see how it all turned out, but I had other things to do, so I ran around to the back of the van and used the key to unlock the door. And when I threw it open there was Professor Meriwether, staring at me, and Mr. McClintock and the other Sea Leopards, and Dr. Little and his friends, and big square-jawed George Sullivan, and Peerless—with both eyes black. Didn't they look surprised, too! I tossed the key to the professor, and in two seconds he was out of his chains and helping the others out of theirs.

Just then the bailiffs broke free from the crowd and came skedaddling back to the van with bruised and bloody faces. They stopped cold when they saw the back door standing wide open, and me with my hand on it; then the driver's face turned red, and he let out a roar and charged at me with his club. At that moment Awkward Morgan jumped out of the van. The driver was big, but Awkward was bigger, and with no trouble at all he jerked the club out of the driver's hand

and broke it over his head. I think the blow might've killed him, but I didn't stick around to find out. As for the other bailiff, when he saw what happened to his friend he suddenly remembered he had to be somewhere else.

The next minute Rosie came running up.

"Come on, everybody!" she said. "Let's go!"

"Go where, young lady?" said Reverend What's-His-Face.

"Reverend," said the professor, "this may not be the best time to ask questions."

The reverend got mad and said he didn't appreciate being told when he could ask questions, and the professor had no right to—but he didn't get to finish, because just then there was a commotion at the far end of the lane, and here comes a whole company of dragoons galloping around the corner on bearwolves, knocking over carts and sending people and dogs scattering in every direction. Franklin was leading the charge—and didn't *he* look steamed up!

Nobody stuck around to see what he wanted; we all took off after Rosie and ran into the alley. Peerless was the last one in, and he went skipping in just as Franklin came charging up on his bearwolf. But its shoulders were too wide for the alley, so all it could do was push its head in and stand there, snarling and snapping at our backs.

We were all strung out in the alley now. I was toward the back, behind Mr. McClintock and Awkward but in front of Peerless. By the time we flew out the other end of the alley Rosie and the others had reached the bridge. I was running so hard I didn't notice that Peerless wasn't behind me until

I was at the gatehouse and heard a shout. I glanced over my shoulder—and there he was, still back at the alley, taunting Franklin with a little victory dance. I couldn't believe it.

Then—BANG!—goes a musket, and down he went.

Everybody ran for cover. Rosie and the others ran into the mausoleum, just on the other side of the bridge, while me and Mr. McClintock and Awkward jumped into the gatehouse. When we looked out we saw Peerless rolling on the ground, howling and clutching his rear; then another shot crashed out, and a musket ball shattered the doorjamb a few inches above my head. Franklin was firing down the alley.

Awkward looked out at the mausoleum.

"We can make it," he said. "Come on!"

"What about Peerless?" I said. "We can't just leave him."

"Why not? He's just getting what he deserves. Come on!"

I looked at Mr. McClintock; he seemed torn.

It just didn't feel right somehow, leaving Peerless behind to die—no matter what he'd done. So I jumped up and ran back to help him. Mr. McClintock shouted at me to come back, but I pretended I couldn't hear him. The next second another shot banged out, and a musket ball went whizzing by my ear, scaring me half to death. I didn't want to get hit, so I cut over and came around to Peerless from the side. By the time I got to him he'd rolled out of the line of fire.

"That jerk shot me in the bum!" he said.

"Gimme your hand," I said. "I'll help you up."

"What?"

"Gimme your hand!"

He gave me his hand, but I couldn't budge him; he was too heavy. Then a shadow fell across us, and when I looked up there was Mr. McClintock and Awkward, come to help. They propped up Peerless between them, and we all started back to the bridge. Suddenly the ground started to tremble, and here comes Franklin charging around the corner at one end of the block with twenty dragoons; at the same moment Colonel Gore came thundering in from the other direction with twenty more. They didn't go straight for us, but aimed for the bridge instead—they wanted to cut us off. Awkward tossed Peerless over his shoulder like he was a sack of beans and the three of us shoved for the bridge as fast as we could go. We went skipping onto it just as the two groups of riders came charging down on us; it was so close I thought I could feel the whiskers of Franklin's bearwolf tickle the back of my neck. Then the bridge shook with a crash as the two groups of riders plowed into each other.

By the time they got themselves untangled and back onto their bearwolves we were at the mausoleum. Dr. Little and the professor took Peerless from Awkward and everyone ran inside. Somebody slammed the doors behind us. There was a big wooden bar to hold them shut with, and it had just been dropped into place when—BOOM!—went the doors.

Franklin was using his bearwolf as a battering ram.

THE RIVER OF WOE

BOOM! went the doors again.

"Those doors won't hold much longer, Orion," Professor Meriwether said. "Do you and your friend here"—he meant Rosie—"have a plan?"

I thought we did, but now I wasn't sure. I looked around the mausoleum. It was a round room with a ceiling shaped like an upside-down bowl. There was a big tomb sitting in the middle of it. This tomb was made out of marble like the rest of the room and had little marble roses on the corners. But I didn't see the secret door that led to the underground river—and that's what I was looking for.

"There's supposed to be a secret door in here," I said.

"All right," he said. "Where does this secret door lead to?"

"An underground river."

The professor looked astonished.

"They were supposed to have it open for us," said Rosie.

"Who was?" said Reverend What's-His-Face.

At that moment a rumbling noise came from underneath the tomb, and it started to slide across the floor. Everybody jumped back. An opening appeared in the floor, and when I peered into it I could see stone steps leading down into the darkness. The next minute a glowing lantern with a bloody little face behind it came bobbing up the steps. It was Glim. Dr. Little hurried over to him and said, "Glim, my dear boy! What happened to your head? Did you crack it?"

"Naw," said Glim. "It's just mushroom ketchup."

The doors boomed again, and a big crack appeared in the wooden bar.

"What're ya waitin' for?" said Glim. "Get in!"

Awkward tossed Peerless over his shoulder and everybody piled down the stairs. At the bottom we found Javelin, and Shivering Jemmy and Fadge, waiting for us. They each had lanterns. Behind them a low tunnel carved out of solid rock stretched away into the darkness.

As soon as everyone was down Javelin told Fadge to close up the opening. There was an iron box built into the wall of the tunnel at the bottom of the steps, and this box had a big lever sticking out of it and two gears connected by a chain. Fadge pulled on the lever, and the tomb rumbled back over the opening. It had just slammed shut when a sudden crash shook the roof of the tunnel, bringing a shower of dust and rocks down on our heads.

"That was too close, Jav!" said Rosie. "You were supposed to have it open for us."

"Sorry about that, Rosie," said Javelin. "Me and the boys was fooling around with the lever and shut the door by mistake. We had a bit o' trouble getting it open again."

"Oh. Well, never mind. Did you get everything?"

"That we did. It's all down at the river."

We heard footsteps over our heads, then, and shouts and other noises that sounded like they were coming from a long way off. The professor said, "Leo, take everyone and follow Orion and his friends to the river. I'll catch up with you."

"What are you going to do?" said Mr. McClintock.

"I want to see if I can disable these gears so our friends up there can't follow us. Would somebody stay back and hold one of these lanterns for me?"

The reverend happened to be standing closest to Professor Meriwether, so he took one of the lanterns and held it for him while the rest of us turned to go down the tunnel. The next second there was a rumbling noise above our heads and the tomb began moving. Light came flooding down the steps from the gap at the top; the barrel of a musket slid through the gap; there was a sudden flash and a BANG!, and as smoke filled the tunnel, the reverend let out a groan and collapsed.

"Leo, get everyone to the river!" the professor roared out. "Awkward, help the doctor with this man!"

Then he grabbed the lever and put all his weight onto it. But the gears kept turning; the colonel and his men must've been pushing on the tomb from above.

"We need something to jam the gears with!" said Rosie.

I dug into my pockets to see if I had anything—the gold sovereign! I ran over to the gearbox and stuck it between the gears. They ground to a stop—and just in time, too; the gap was almost wide enough for a man to squeeze through.

Awkward and Dr. Little had dragged the reverend out of the line of fire by this time. The doctor did what he could for him, but that wasn't much, considering how he was already dead. So we left him there and hurried to catch up with the others. The tunnel ran straight for about a quarter of a mile and then began to slope down. Not long after that we heard a noise up ahead. It sounded like a dull kind of roar, and it got louder as we went along. At last we came out into a big cavern. This cavern had a river running through the middle of it, and at the edge of this river there was a jetty with four jolly boats tied up to it—and one of them, I was surprised to see, was the *Lady Jane*. They had patched her up and put a fresh coat of paint on her.

The king was there, with Tricky Dick, and Spithead, and Cracker and the rest of the flimps. He said, "Step this way, ladies and gentlemen. Here's your boats, and over here you got everything you'll need for your voyage down the river."

He had a pile of provisions there for us. There were hams, and pies, and boxes of green apples, and loaves of bread, and two cases of moss-cider to wash it all down with. Dr. Little's medical bag was there, too. Javelin had gone to Mrs. Jopson's house while I was sleeping on the sofa and gotten it from her, along with a basket of roly-polies she made special for me.

The professor was beyond surprised.

"If this doesn't beat all," he said. "Well, I suppose there's nothing for us to do now but climb aboard and shove off."

"There is one thing, actually" said Mr. McClintock. "We only need one of these boats. We ought to scuttle the other three so we can't be followed."

Professor Meriwether said it was a good idea, but then we discovered that we didn't have anything to scuttle them with. The planks were so thick we would've needed a power drill to make a hole in them, and nobody had thought to bring one. So we did the only thing we could do—we untied them and pushed them out into the river. The current swept them a hundred or so yards downstream, where they got wedged in among some boulders on the other side.

There wasn't anything we could do about it, so we loaded our provisions into the *Lady Jane* and climbed aboard. Rosie got in with us. That surprised me; she'd never said anything about wanting to escape with us. But she wanted to come, she said, and nobody could think of a good reason why she shouldn't. When we were ready to go we hung a lantern in the bow; then we said good-bye to the king and Javelin and Glim and the rest of them and rowed out into the river.

Before long the current grabbed us and began to carry us downstream. It swept us along at a pretty good clip, so we shipped our oars and settled in for the ride. Baldy took the tiller, while Dr. Little got out a scalpel and dug the musket ball out of Peerless's bum. I never heard such yowling; you would've thought he was being murdered. I couldn't stand it, so I went up to the bow with Rosie. On both sides of the river we could see a low rocky bank sliding by; but when we looked ahead, or up, or behind all we could see was a solid wall of darkness.

After the musket ball had been dug out of Peerless's rear end—and he'd finally stopped bawling—everyone wanted to know how we'd pulled off the rescue. So me and Rosie took turns telling the story. When I came to the part where the warden gave me the gold sovereign to keep my mouth shut Dr. Little's face just glowed with satisfaction, and Professor Meriwether slapped his knee and laughed so hard the tears rolled down his cheeks. We ate breakfast after that, and then for a long time nobody said anything—I figured they were too busy thinking about what a close call they'd just had— and the only sound I could hear was the river gurgling and babbling through the cavern.

Another hour or so passed by, and I was beginning to feel pretty comfortable and drowsy, on account of my stomach being half-full of roly-polies, when all of a sudden Rosie sat up and said, "Listen!"

I came wide-awake; so did everybody else. At first I didn't hear anything unusual; just the river babbling along. Then I made out a roaring noise coming out of the darkness ahead. As the current swept us along it got louder and louder. The river seemed to be getting narrower, too. Then—

"Look!" someone shouted. "To starboard!"

Up ahead there was a big rock sticking out of the river. It had a board lashed to it, and painted on this board in bright red letters were the words "DANGER AHEAD! KEEP RIGHT!" In another minute the rock slid past us and was swallowed up by the darkness astern.

"Everyone to your oars!" said Professor Meriwether.

We jumped to our oars and rowed as if our lives depended on it—which they did, for all I knew. Baldy tried to steer us over to the right-hand side of the river, but by this time the current was sweeping us along so fast that we got carried a mile downstream before we could crab fifty yards over. The roar got louder and louder; before long it seemed to fill the whole cavern. Then another rock came racing up out of the darkness—only in a minute we saw that it wasn't a rock at all, but a wall dividing the river into two branches. Before we could crab over to the right side of it the current swept us down the left branch. It wouldn't do any good to keep rowing now, so we shipped our oars and waited to see what would happen next. I was pretty sure it wouldn't be good.

Minutes passed by; then Mr. Clark pointed at something up ahead and said, "What in God's name is that?"

I looked—but I wish I hadn't. Up ahead a line of jagged rocks stretched across the river, like gigantic fangs. Some of them jutted down from the roof of the cavern; others stuck up out of the water. It looked like we were being swept into the mouth of a ginormous crocodile. The professor roared, "Get down!", and the next thing I know here comes a great big rock flying up at us. Somebody put a hand on my head and shoved me into the bilge; there was a jarring crash, and as I shot across the bottom of the boat and slammed into a bulkhead there was a noise like glass shattering and we were plunged into the blackest kind of darkness.

We went crashing from one rock to another till our teeth were almost rattled out of our heads. Sometimes we would crash into them head-on, then go bouncing off; other times the boat would get spun around and we'd crash into them sideways. That was the worst, because then the river would drive the *Lady Jane* right up the side of the rock, and I just knew she was going to swamp—and then I'd drown in that awful roaring darkness, deep under the earth, and for the rest of his life my grampa would wonder why I never came home. But she always managed to work herself free; then off we'd go again, and crash into more rocks. It was like being inside a barrel that was hurtling down the side of a mountain—oh, and there's fifteen other people in the barrel with you, too.

At long last the crashing stopped, and soon afterward we left the roaring behind us. The river seemed to be slowing down and getting wider again, but we couldn't be sure because our lantern had gotten smashed when we crashed into that first rock. Everybody was bruised, and sore, and wet to the skin, but except for me no one had any serious injuries. The back of my hand had gotten burned when hot oil from the lantern splashed across it. I'd been so scared at the time I hadn't noticed, but you can bet I noticed it now. Dr. Little slathered some kind of jelly on the burn, which helped ease the pain, and then he bandaged up my hand.

Two or three hours crawled by after that, only in the dark it seemed more like two or three days. I'd just about made up my mind that I was never going to see the sun again when Rosie noticed a glow up ahead. It got brighter as we drifted toward it, and pretty soon we could make out the banks of the river again. Half an hour later we floated around a bend and into a big sea cave. The mouth of this cave was over a hundred feet high, and when I looked out through it I saw glittering green water and a patch of blue sky.

Then we saw something that made us catch our breaths. On the far side of the cave, toward the back, there were two tall ships riding on their anchors. Both of them were painted white from stem to stern—even their masts and spars were white. And when I saw that I knew that one of them was the ship that came and took Henry Collins away.

Professor Meriwether stood up, looking all wonder-struck, and said, "Gentlemen, unless I'm greatly mistaken those are the legendary lost ships of John Franklin's expedition."

HMS *EREBUS*

WE busted out our oars and rowed over to the ships. Their names were *Erebus* and *Terror*, just like the two mountains. And that's when it finally clicked—"the Terror" that Henry Collins had those nightmares about wasn't a mountain or a monster, but a *ship*. I could see why, too; just one look at her was enough to send shivers down my spine. Her figurehead was a charging bearwolf with its fangs bared, and her white hull and spars, all covered with frost and hung with icicles, threw off an eerie glow in the gloom of the sea cave. To be chased by a ship like that through ice and fog and storms for months on end would've given anybody nightmares.

The *Erebus* was just as scary. Baldy said both ships looked a little too much like the *Flying Dutchman* for his taste; he said he'd sooner swim home than step aboard either one. But we had to go aboard one of them if we wanted to get home. The only question was, Which one? It didn't seem to matter; they looked the same in every way. Both ships had iron plates bolted to their hulls to protect them from sea ice, and both had cannons for fighting battles at sea and steam engines for maneuvering around floes when there wasn't enough wind to sail. So I said why don't we flip for it. Everyone said that was a good idea, and so I took out one of my silver pennies and we flipped for it. *Erebus* it was.

When we got aboard her we discovered that her hold was full of provisions: salted cod, and dried seal meat, and what they call "hard tack," which is a sort of biscuit that tastes like sawdust, and fresh water, and parkas and caps, and muskets, and ammunition for the muskets, and cannons and cannon-balls; and tons of coal for the steam engine. In the cabin we found charts, and compasses, and logbooks, and cigars, and brandy to go with the cigars, and just about everything else we could want for a sea voyage. We even found tobacco for the professor's pipe.

After we had a look around the professor called everyone to the quarterdeck—that's the deck where the wheel is—and announced he was putting Mr. McClintock in charge of the ship. From then on we couldn't call him *Mister* McClintock, but only *Captain* McClintock, and we had to do whatever he told us. He didn't fool around, either, the new captain, but clapped his hands behind his back and began throwing out orders left and right. In no time everybody had a job to do and was hurrying away to do it—the Sea Leopards into the rigging to learn how to work the sails; Mr. Pilkington to the capstan to figure out how to raise the anchor; Mr. Clark to the engine room to fire up the boiler; Baldy to the galley to make lunch; George Sullivan to the cargo hold to bring up parkas and gloves and caps; Mr. Honey and Mr. Brown to the stern to hoist the *Lady Jane* aboard; and Dr. Little and Rosie to the sick bay with Peerless. Baldy didn't say I had to help him, so I went to the cabin with the professor and Mr. McClintock—Captain McClintock, I mean—to study the charts. While we were there the captain brought up the idea of blowing up the *Terror*, but Professor Meriwether said an explosion inside the cave might bring the roof down on our heads. That was too bad; I would've liked to see it.

By late that afternoon we were ready to put to sea. It took Awkward and George and seven of the other strongest men aboard, heaving with all their might on the capstan bars, to pull the anchor free of the bottom; but finally it came up, trailing seaweed and dripping clumps of mud. The captain gave the order to stoke the boiler, and the next thing I knew the *Terror* was sliding past to starboard, and Charlie Button was leaning over the gunwale with the lead line and singing out, "Eleven fathoms, mud!" and the water beneath the ship was turning from black to green. A minute later we steamed out of the cave and into the afternoon sun. The sea spread away to the horizon, all green and glittery, and everywhere we looked we could see whitecaps whipped up by the breeze. There was a headland a few miles to the east of us, and the minute we got around it and out into the swell the captain gave the order to blow down the boiler and unfurl the sails. The Sea Leopards flicked their cigars over the side and went swarming into the rigging like so many monkeys, and in no time the sails were flashing out and filling with wind, and the spars were bending under the strain, and the water began to race along the hull. We were finally on our way home.

It didn't take long for Baldy to change his mind about the *Erebus*. He admitted that in the light of day she didn't look at all like the *Flying Dutchman*, and he enjoyed sailing her so much that I could hardly ever get a turn at the wheel.

In the meantime Rosie and all the other colonists except Dr. Little turned green and had to be helped below to their bunks; none of them had ever been to sea, and it didn't seem to agree with them. Later that night when Baldy rang the bell for dinner none of them came. I took a bowl of seal blubber stew in to Rosie, but for some reason she didn't want it.

The professor spent most of his time in the cabin, going through the ship's logbooks. There were dozens of them— great big slab-like things with sealskin covers and pages that smelled like old wine and stale tobacco—and they had every detail of every voyage the *Erebus* had ever made, going back almost two hundred years. After dinner I made the mistake of poking my head into the cabin to see how he was coming along. When he noticed me he said, "Ah, Orion! There you are. Come in, come in. You've got to hear this." So I went in, and he read to me from those logbooks until I thought my ears were going to fall off. Sometimes it would be interesting, like when they talked about how they hunted whales or sailed to Greenland to look for wives. But mostly it was the driest, dullest kind of stuff, like how thick the ice was in this or that place, or what direction the wind was blowing and so on. He would've kept me there all night if Dr. Little hadn't stuck his head in and told me to go to bed.

The nice weather stayed with us the rest of that night and throughout the next day. By the end of the second day Rosie and all the other colonists had gotten over their seasickness and were up and about again. The only person who wasn't up and about was Peerless. He claimed he was still too weak to leave the sick bay, but if you ask me he just wanted to get out of doing his share of the work. As for me, I was starting to think about how nice it would be to see my grampa once again, and hang out with Dell Robbins and my other friends. After what I'd just been through school wouldn't seem nearly so bad, either; I might get picked on every now and then, but at least nothing there would try to eat me.

So the first two days ran along, like I said, with everything going great guns. Then on the morning of the third day we ran into some fog. It was patchy; one minute we'd be in it, and we couldn't see the bowsprit from the wheel; the next we'd be out of it, and we could. The *Erebus* had no radar, so the captain posted a lookout in the crow's nest—we didn't want to sail into an iceberg, after all.

Later that afternoon I was sitting on the capstan with Rosie, trying to explain to her who Doctor Doom was, when all of a sudden the lookout hollered, "Sail ho!"

"Where away?" cried the captain.

"Dead astern!"

We jumped down off the capstan and ran aft along with everybody else. There was a heavy fogbank a couple of miles behind us. I stared at it, but all I could see was fog. Captain McClintock asked the lookout if he was sure.

"I think so!" was the answer.

The next second Rosie said, "I see it!"

There was a kind of whirlwind in the fog—and then a tall ship came crashing out of the mist, trailing wisps of fog from her spars and looking like a furious ghost.

It was the *Terror*.

THE SEA CHASE

SHE was booming right along, flying every last scrap of sail she could carry and throwing off great big sheets of foaming green water from her bow. I got out the spyglass. There was Franklin all right, in his long blue coat and funny admiral's hat, leaning over the rail and studying us with *his* spyglass. Spartacus was on one side of him, with his paws on the rail and his tongue flapping in the breeze, and Colonel Gore was on the other, with *his* paws on the rail. They weren't alone, either; the decks were crowded with dragoons.

"Well, Captain?" said Professor Meriwether. "What would you suggest we do now?"

"Run," said Captain McClintock.

So we ran. Every sail we had was brought up to the deck and hoisted, and everyone took hold of a sheet and helped.

Out flashed the flying jib, and the main and mizzen topgallant staysails; out flashed the skysail, and the moonsail, and the spanker, and other sails I'd never heard of. As the wind caught them they cracked out like pistol shots and stretched the sheets so tight they felt like iron bars. A kind of shudder went through the *Erebus*, and she shot over the waves like a thoroughbred out of the gate.

But even with our extra speed the *Terror* gained on us. At first we couldn't figure out why. She wasn't any bigger than the *Erebus*, and she was flying the same sails. How come she was sailing so much faster? At last the captain said, "Why, of course! It's as plain as noon. Orion, run down to the engine room and ask Mr. Clark to come up."

So down I go to the engine room, where I find Mr. Clark with his head in the boiler. When I said the captain wanted to see him he pulled it out and followed me back up to the deck, grumbling about how he never got a moment's peace to do his work. And then, when he sees the captain, he says, pretty gruff, "Well? What is it now?"

"How much coal do we have aboard?" said the captain.

"About seventeen and a half tons. I'd like more, but unless it drops out of the sky I don't see how I'll get it. Why?"

"How is it stored?"

"In iron scuttles. Eighteen of 'em. Why?"

"I want you to dump it overboard—scuttles and all."

Mr. Clark looked surprised. "How am I supposed to run my engine with no coal?" he said.

"You're not. We need to lighten the ship."

"Well, then find something else to get rid of."

"It's the heaviest thing aboard, Jim. It has to go."

"No, Leo—I won't do it!"

"Yes, Jim—you will."

"Oh, all right!"

And he whipped out his rag and stomped off, polishing his head. The Sea Leopards rigged a hoist to the mainmast, and before long great big iron scuttles with coal dust streaming off of them were being hoisted out of the hold and dropped over the side. Mr. Clark supervised from below; you could see him down there, through the hatch, buffing his dome.

By the time the last scuttle went overboard the *Terror* was only a mile and a half behind us—and still gaining. So the captain ordered us to throw overboard everything that wasn't nailed down—including all the cannons, except for the two smaller ones at the bow—and pump out all but a ton of our fresh water. He even ordered us to swing the *Lady Jane* over the side and cut her loose. I was sorry to see her treated like that, after all she'd done to get us safely down the river.

But even after all that the *Terror* still gained on us. So the captain called Mr. Clark back up to the deck.

"We need to take more weight off her, Jim," he says.

"Well," says Mr. Clark, all sour-like, "then take it off."

"There's only one thing left to throw overboard."

"Besides yourself, you mean?"

"This isn't a time for jokes, Jim. The engine has to go."

Mr. Clark gave a little jump. "The engine!" he said. "You can't mean it."

"It's of no use to us now that the coal's gone."

"And whose fault is that? No, Leo—I won't do it!"

"Yes, Jim—you will."

"No, I won't!"

"You will."

"Won't!"

"Will!"

"Oh, all right!"

And off he went again, this time polishing his head so hard it looked like he'd take the skin clean off. When he got back to the engine room he began to take the engine apart, and as each piece came off the Sea Leopards hoisted it up through the hatch and—KERPLUNK!—over the side it went. It was a big job, and by the time the last piece splashed into the sea the sun had sunk below the horizon. The *Terror* was only a mile behind us now, but at least she wasn't gaining on us any longer. That was good, because we had no more dead weight to throw overboard—except maybe Peerless.

Not long afterward the moon came up as big and bright as I'd ever seen it. Everybody was hungry after all that work, so the captain told Baldy to make supper, and then he and the professor and Dr. Little headed down to the cabin. Me and Rosie went with them. In the cabin the captain spread a chart out on the table, and said, "I'm afraid we don't have many options, gentlemen."

"Can't we outrun them?" said the professor.

"No, I don't think so. We're too shorthanded to beat them in a long sea chase. Eventually they'll catch up to us."

"So we'll fight them."

"Professor," said Dr. Little, "Franklin has sixty or seventy men with him, many of them professional sharpshooters and gunners. There are just sixteen of us, and that includes a man with a gunshot wound and two youngsters. If we try to fight them we'll be massacred."

"He's right, Charles," said Captain McClintock. "We can't fight them, and we can't outrun them."

"All right," said the professor, "what *can* we do?"

"We can hide."

"Hide! Where?"

The captain put his finger on the chart. "Here," he said.

Everybody crowded around him and looked at the chart. Thirty miles southeast of the island there was a patch of sea marked in red, and beside it was a drawing of a sinking ship inside a circle of skulls with the words "DEVIL'S GRAVEYARD: TREACHEROUS! KEEP OUT!" written under it. The hair on the back of my neck stood up when I read that, because Devil's Graveyard was the name of that creepy place Henry Collins had raved about at the cove.

But Professor Meriwether wasn't scared. When he saw the drawing he got excited and started to rummage through the stack of logbooks. "I read about this place in one of the logbooks," he said. "Which one was it, now? No, not that one. Ah, yes, this is the one. It was toward the back, I think. Oh, here it is. Listen to this. This entry was written by Captain Fitzjames on May 23, 1883:

'Today I completed the circumnavigation of a seemingly permanent bank of fog roughly 8 & 1/2 leagues SE of New Britain. Called the Devil's Graveyard be-cause of the numerous ships that have ventured inside & were never seen again, it appears to be a region of perpetual fog & gloom, with sea ice & icebergs present year-round. Strange, unsettling noises & an evil-smelling odor emanate from the fog, for which I can conceive no natural explanation. The sight of that ominous mist brings to mind Dante's warning: Omnes relinquite spes, o vos intrantes.'"

"What does that mean?" I said.

"It's Latin," said Rosie. "It means 'Abandon all hope, you who enter here.'"

I didn't know if I ought to be scared, or impressed by the fact that Rosie knew Latin. Probably both.

"If our wind holds we should get there before dawn," said the captain. "We can hide out in the fog until nightfall, and then sneak out under cover of darkness. With some luck we could be over the horizon before the moon comes up. Does anyone have any objections?"

I could think of one or two, but I kept them to myself. The professor and Dr. Little liked the captain's plan, so he sent Rosie up to the deck with the order to change course. Then he said, "Doctor, didn't you tell me that one of your fellow colonists has some knowledge of the ship's guns?"

"That would be George Sullivan," said the doctor. "One of his ancestors was a gunner aboard this ship."

So the captain sent me to fetch George. He was surprised when I told him the captain wanted to see him, and on our way down to the cabin he wrung his cap and asked me if I knew what it was about. He looked easier when I told him I thought it had something to do with guns.

When we got to the cabin the captain asked George how much he knew about the ship's guns.

"Quite a bit, sir, as it happens," said George. "My great-great-grandfather was a gunner aboard this ship. Everything he knew about her guns he wrote down in his journals—how to load 'em, how to clean 'em, how to take 'em apart and put 'em back together again—everything. I found them journals under some rubbish in the attic when I was a boy not much older than Orion here, sir, and read 'em cover to cover. Mrs. Sullivan read 'em too, and she knows as much about guns as I do. Now I think on it, she said to me one day, 'Georgie, luv, did you know you could use a slow-match to—' "

"Thank you, Mr. Sullivan," the captain cut in. "There are two cannons at the bow. Can they be moved aft?"

"The long nines? Oh yes, sir. Just so as you brace 'em up good and tight. Are you thinkin' of taking a few shots at the

Terror, sir? Those nine-pound cannonballs can do a fair bit of damage if aimed proper."

I'd like to aim one at Franklin's head, I thought, and see what kind of damage it would do. Probably take it clean off.

"Perhaps," said the captain. "I understand that we have a supply of muskets aboard. Are you familiar with them?"

"I am, sir, as it happens. I had an old Brown Bess before Lord Franklin made owning guns illegal. Mrs. Sullivan had one, too. She's a better shot than I am."

"Is she? It's a shame she's not here. We could use her."

"You think it'll come to blows, sir?"

"I hope not, Mr. Sullivan, but we have to be ready in case it does. See that those cannons are moved aft, and then bring up a round score of muskets and show the men how to use them. Let them fire off a few practice rounds."

"Yes, sir. Should I bring up the other weapons, too?"

"The other weapons?"

"Yes, sir. The armory's fairly overflowing with 'em. There's pistols, and cutlasses, and swords, and grappling hooks, and smoke bombs, and pikes—you name it. There's even a box of grenadoes down there, now I think on it."

The captain said all right, and George left to carry out his orders. Me and Rosie wanted to go with him and help, but at that moment Baldy knocked on the door and said supper was on the table. When we got done eating we went up to the deck to see how George was coming along. He'd already moved the two cannons back to the quarterdeck, and now he was showing everybody how to load and fire their muskets;

even Peerless had come up from the sick bay to see what all the hullabaloo was about. There were a few dozen muskets stacked up behind the deckhouse, along with pistols and all kinds of other weapons for fighting a battle with; there was even a box of grenadoes (grenadoes are little round bombs that people throw at each other). Me and Rosie each picked out a pistol, and George showed us how to fire them. Then we went over to the stern rail and for the next hour or so we blazed away at the *Terror* along with everybody else. She was out of range, but it was fun anyway—and didn't Rosie's eyes flash every time she let Franklin have it!

Through the rest of that night the *Terror* chased us across the silvery sea. Sometimes she'd come to within half a mile; other times she'd fall back to a mile. Around midnight she pulled closer than ever before; you could see her back there, hull down and black against the stars, tearing across the sea. Suddenly a flash lit up the horizon; a few seconds later there was a dull kind of BOOM! in the distance, and here comes a cannonball smashing through the cabin window and knocks the professor's pipe right out of his mouth. He stormed up to the deck, madder than a box of bees, and told the captain he wanted to fire back. The captain said gladly, so I fetched George up from below, and he and the professor blazed away at the *Terror* with the two cannons until they were too hot to touch. Most of their shots fell short, but later we found out that one of them had punched a hole in the *Terror's* jib. It was almost three in the morning before Dr. Little finally came over and told me and Rosie we had to go to bed.

Toward dawn a commotion on the deck woke us up. We were about to throw on our parkas and go up to see what all the fuss was about when Cam Hoffer came bounding down the companionway and said, "Quick, come see!"

"Come see what?" said me and Rosie at the same time.

"What d'ya think? The Devil's Graveyard!"

IN THE DEVIL'S GRAVEYARD

WE threw on our parkas and hurried up to the deck. Ahead there was a solid wall of fog stretching across the horizon. It wasn't your ordinary old fog that's white or gray, but a dark, smoky kind of fog; so dark it looked almost black. As for the *Terror*, she was now closer than ever. I got the spyglass, and Rosie and me took turns watching Franklin as he paced the quarterdeck, looking as if he couldn't wait to get his hands around our throats, until Baldy rang the bell for breakfast.

When we came back on deck the fog towered over us like a cliff, and not long after that we sailed into it. There wasn't any gradualness to it at all—one minute we were booming along with the sun on our faces; the next we were ghosting through the thickest, coldest, darkest kind of gloom. It was like somebody had snatched away the sun and left a candle in its place. When we got about a mile into the fog Captain McClintock put the ship on a new course and ordered total silence. From then on we couldn't slam any doors, or laugh out loud, or go clomping up and down the companionway, or holler down through the hatch to ask Baldy when lunch would be ready; and if we wanted to say anything we had to whisper. I climbed out onto the bowsprit with Rosie and we sat there, with our legs dangling over the water, and listened to the fog. Sometimes we'd hear a noise that sounded like giant barrels rolling down stairs, and we knew that part of an iceberg had broken off and slid down into the sea; at other times we'd hear a thundering kind of noise followed by a big WHOOSH! and we knew an iceberg had capsized somewhere close by. We heard other noises, too; strange, creepy noises that sounded like children whispering and giggling, and one that sounded like someone wailing. Once I looked into the water and thought I saw faces staring back at me. It gave me a nasty jolt, and after that I didn't look into the water again.

We stayed up there for the rest of that morning, watching the fog and listening for the *Terror*, but there was no sign of her anywhere—only every time an iceberg drifted out of the fog I *thought* it was her. Once we heard a splash that started my heart racing; but nothing ever came of it, and we never found out what it was. That was fine by me—I didn't want to know.

Toward noon I left Rosie at the bowsprit and went to see how Baldy was coming along with lunch. The professor was at the wheel with the captain, while George and Awkward were leaning on the rail, smoking cigars and staring out into the fog—and everybody being as quiet as mice.

Well, I was about to head below when here came Peerless clomping up the companionway steps, acting like he owned the place. When he got to the deck he stood there a minute, scratching himself; then he goes over to Awkward and says, in his regular loud voice, "Bum a stogie off yah, mate?"

"Keep it down!" Awkward hissed. "Are you trying to give us away?"

Peerless's face went dark, and there might've been trouble if George hadn't stepped between them and said we were all shipmates now, and should be friendly and civil toward one another if we could. Then he offered Peerless one of his own cigars. Peerless snatched it up and walked off in a huff.

The show was pretty much over, so I went on down to the galley and asked Baldy if he needed any help. He said lunch was already on the table, and I could help by going back up and telling everyone who wasn't on duty to come down nice and quiet—he didn't want to ring the bell, you see. So back up I go and tell everyone, in a whisper, that lunch was ready and to come down nice and quiet. I found Peerless slouching against the deckhouse, smoking his cigar and looking sore, and when I told him that lunch was ready he threw his cigar over his shoulder and headed for the companionway. I was just starting after him when I heard a hissing noise coming from behind the deckhouse, where we kept the muskets and other weapons. I hurried around to see what it was—so did Awkward and George—and wouldn't you know it, of all the places that Peerless's cigar could have gone, it had landed in the box of grenadoes—and touched off one of the fuses!

George grabbed the box and flung it over the rail with all his strength. Awkward shouted, "Take cover!"—and as him and George dove one way and I the other, the box exploded with a BOOM! that was so loud they must've heard it halfway to the moon. The sound of the blast went rumbling into the fog like thunder rolling across the sky.

The explosion blew out a twenty-foot section of the gunwale, but luckily no one got hurt. But someone was about to be, because now Awkward jumped up, looking like a volcano that was ready to blow, and said, "That's it!"

Then he sprang at Peerless. Down they went—Awkward with his hands wrapped around Peerless's throat, and Peerless clawing at Awkward's face—and both of them making enough noise to wake a dead cat. It took George and Baldy and all the rest of the Sea Leopards to pull them apart. And they'd only just gotten them apart, too, when all of a sudden Rosie came running up and said, "Quiet, everyone! Listen!"

Everyone froze. I held my breath and listened, but the only sound I could hear was the water swirling past the hull. Oh, and my heart thumping—I could hear that.

Then a noise drifted out of the fog; it was that faint kind of fluttering noise a sail makes when it flaps in the breeze. A moment later a shout came from the crow's nest. "Ship ho! Starboard quarter!"

We all ran over to the rail—and there was the *Terror*, all grim and ghostly, gliding up out of the fog! Before Captain

McClintock could give out any orders she was alongside us, so close we could see the sooty faces of her gunners as they stared along the barrels of their cannons at us. The captain roared, "Everyone get down!"; the next second there was an awful thundering crash, and as I hit the deck fire and smoke came squirting out of the *Terror's* gun ports.

I threw my arms over my head; then I heard a noise like a tree snapping in half and something came crashing down all around me. But I couldn't see what it was; there was too much smoke. I could *hear* just fine, though—shouts, and screams, and the steady POP! POP! and BANG! BANG! BANG! of pistol and musket fire.

Then all at once the din stopped and it was quiet again. I eased my head up and looked around. There was a cloud of smoke drifting across the deck, and through it I could make out the foremast lying over the starboard rail in a tangle of shattered spars and shredded sails. Men were getting up out of the wreckage and stumbling around; they looked dazed and confused, like they'd been in a car crash. Dr. Little was picking his way through the wreckage, seeing who was hurt and doing what he could for them. When he spotted Rosie and me he hurried over and asked us if we were all right. We said we were.

The next minute the captain came running up and asked Dr. Little if anyone had been hurt.

"Pilkington's dead," said Dr. Little. "He was struck on the head by the foremast. Killed instantly, poor chap. Otherwise just cuts and splinter wounds. We were lucky."

Mr. Pilkington wasn't, I thought. And he'd been so nice to me, too, helping me look for my cap in the courtroom. I felt sorry for his wife, even though I didn't know her from a bean, and angry at Peerless for being such a jerk and giving us away. I almost wished I'd left him back at the alley.

Professor Meriwether came over now. Part of his ear had been shot off, but he didn't seem to care; he was too mad.

"We've got to ram her, Leo!" he said.

"Ram her!" said the captain. "You mean—"

"Yes—take 'em by surprise! Franklin won't be expecting it. Well? What do you think?"

"I like it! It's bold."

"Good. Get the ship into position, and I'll rally the men. Doctor, would you please come with me? And you two"—he looked at me and Rosie—"get below and stay there!"

Then he hurried off with Dr. Little to round everyone up and lay out the plan. Everybody was for it—nobody wanted to just sit there and wait for Franklin to swing back around and blow us to Kingdom Come. In no time at all everyone was grabbing muskets, and shoving pistols under their belts, and snatching up cutlasses, and pikes, and boarding axes—whatever they wanted; there was plenty of everything to go around. Awkward and George each took a hammer. These weren't your ordinary hammers, either, but great big things with handles almost three feet long and studded iron heads that weighed fifteen pounds, like Thor has.

Meantime the captain found Peerless and ordered him to take the wheel.

"I'm joining the boarding party, Jones," he said. "When I give the word, throw the wheel hard to port and bring her head around until she's pointed at the *Terror*. You've got to hit her dead on, do you understand? We mean to board her over the bowsprit."

Peerless said he understood, and then the captain hurried forward to join the boarding party. On the way he noticed me and Rosie still hanging out by the deckhouse. He got all mad, then, and asked us if we hadn't heard the professor tell us to go below—because *he* had. So we cleared out down the companionway. But I wasn't about to miss the action; so the minute I heard him go away I started back up.

"Where are you going?" said Rosie.

"Back up," I said. "I can't see a thing from down here."

"Then I'm coming with you."

"The professor told you to stay below."

"The professor told *us* to stay below."

"I think he meant you, mainly."

"Because I'm a girl, you mean?"

"Well—"

Boy, didn't her eyes flash then! It was all she could do to keep from flying at me. I wish I'd never said it; I didn't know her very well then, or I never would've. She was the bravest girl that ever lived—and still is. Anyway, she pushed by me and went back up the companionway. I slunk up after her, feeling pretty sheepish.

We peeped out over the deckhouse. There was Professor Meriwether, and Captain McClintock, and the doctor and the rest of them, all crouched down in the bow and armed to the teeth. And there was the *Terror*, fifty yards off our port bow and closing fast. She was sailing close to a big iceberg.

Suddenly—BANG! BANG! BANG!—a burst of musket fire broke out from high in the *Terror*'s rigging, and as me and Rosie pulled our heads behind the deckhouse a musket ball smacked into the gunwale behind us.

"Now, Jones!" shouted the captain. "Hard to port!"

Nothing happened.

"Jones! Hard to port—NOW!"

Still nothing.

Why isn't he turning, I wondered? So I looked aft to see what the matter was—and there was no one at the wheel!

I saw that by the time anybody else could get back to the wheel it would be too late, so I jumped up and hightailed it to the quarterdeck. When I got there I found out what the problem was—Peerless was cowering behind a barrel. With bullets flying all around me I grabbed the wheel and threw it over; the next second there was a tremendous crash and I was thrown to the deck. I heard a strange, thundering noise that I couldn't account for; and then the professor and the rest of them jumped up with a wild yell and went swarming across the bowsprit onto the *Terror*.

THE BATTLE FOR THE *TERROR*

SHE was lying directly across our bow, with her quarterdeck under our bowsprit and the rest of her hidden under a cloud of smoke. And coming out of that smoke was the most fearsome commotion I'd ever heard—swords clashing, and men roaring, and muskets crashing out—and everywhere flashes of light from guns going off. As for that thundering noise, I saw now what was causing it: the collision had slammed the *Terror* against the side of the iceberg, bringing tons of snow and ice avalanching down on top of her.

I jumped up and raced up to the bow to get a better look. But what I got instead was a big surprise, because there was Rosie, with a pistol in one hand and a wicked-looking knife in the other, making her way across the bowsprit and onto the *Terror*. And didn't she look fierce! I called after her and asked her what she thought she was doing. She said she had a score to settle, then before I could tell her not to be stupid and to come back she jumped down off the bowsprit onto the *Terror*'s quarterdeck and disappeared into the smoke.

Dang it, I thought; now I've *got* to go.

So I raced back to the deckhouse and grabbed a couple of pistols out of the stack. Then I ran back up to the bow and started across the bowsprit to the *Terror*. Her decks were still hidden in smoke; I couldn't see Rosie anywhere.

Well, I was just about to jump down onto the *Terror* and go look for her when a gap opened up in the smoke—and there was Dr. Little, with his back against the wheel and a cutlass in his hand, trying to fight off three dragoons. All at once they let out a yell and rushed him, and the last thing I saw before the smoke closed over them was Dr. Little going down under a heap of dragoons. I forgot about Rosie—and about how scared I was, too—and the next thing I knew I was jumping off the bowsprit, with both of my pistols out, and running headlong into the smoke to help the doctor.

And then I crashed into somebody.

I was so startled I didn't recognize him at first; and then I see it's Downing, the dragoon who turned tail and ran away that time we surprised each other in the fog back in Maine. This time he didn't run away, but just showed me a mouthful of crooked yellow teeth and raised his pistol.

But I raised both of mine faster. I aimed them at his chest and squeezed the triggers. CLICK! CLICK!

I'd forgotten to cock them!

Downing laughed the wildest kind of laugh and aimed his pistol at my head. I shut my eyes; I didn't want to watch my own head get blown off. Then—

BANG!

I opened my eyes. My head was still on! I couldn't believe it. Meantime Downing looked like he'd had the surprise of his life; then he dropped his pistol and fell over dead. When I looked around to see who'd shot him here comes George Sullivan stepping out of the smoke, with his hammer in one hand and a smoking pistol in the other. I was never happier to see anybody in my life. He told me to try to remember to cock my pistols the next time, and then he ran back into the smoke to help Dr. Little.

I figured he could handle the dragoons with that monster hammer of his, so I went to look for Rosie. Well, what with all the musket balls whizzing past my head, and the smoke getting in my eyes, and the people suddenly appearing out of nowhere and just as suddenly disappearing again, and the shocking noise and all, I forgot to watch where I was going, and the next minute I tumbled off the quarterdeck and fell onto the main deck below.

I bounced back up as quick as I could and looked around. I was standing in front of a companionway, with smoke all around me. Somehow I still had the pistols in my hands.

Just then a man came staggering out of the smoke with a bloody arm hanging at his side. It was Mr. Brown, and when he noticed me he fell onto his knees and stretched his hand out toward me. I reached for it, but before I could grab it

Colonel Gore came marching up out of the smoke and ran him through with his sword.

I let out a cry; I couldn't help it.

The colonel saw me, and he raised his sword and charged at me. He had such a wild look in his eyes that for a second I forgot I had a couple of loaded pistols in my hands. Then I remembered—and this time I didn't forget to cock them.

BANG! they both went.

The recoil from the pistols lifted me off my feet and sent me flying backwards through companionway, and I hit the floor at the bottom of the stairs so hard that the wind was knocked out of me. The sense must have been knocked out, too, because for a while I didn't know where I was, or why I was on the floor, or whose body that was slumped over the threshold at the top of the stairs. And then I saw the sword in its hand, and it all came back to me.

I didn't get a chance to celebrate my victory, because just then Franklin, with a bloody sword in his hand and a pistol in his belt, appeared in the doorway at the top of the steps. When he saw Colonel Gore lying there dead, and me at the bottom of the stairs with two smoking pistols in my hands, he let out a roar and bounded down the steps. I dropped the pistols and tried to get away from him, but I got backed up against a post, and before I knew it he was on me. Up went his sword; then he aimed a blow at me that would've sliced me clean in half, if it hadn't been intercepted by the post.

I didn't wait for him to try again, but jumped to my feet and took off like Skeletor himself was after me. I ran down a kind of corridor between two rows of cannons and into a cabin. The floor of this cabin was littered with broken glass, and papers, and charts, and logbooks, and overturned tables and chairs, and where one of the walls should've been there was nothing but a big gaping hole.

I locked the door, and ran over to the hole and looked out. Fifteen feet below me there was an ice floe that had drifted out of the fog and was bumping against the side of the ship. But I couldn't see how I could get down to it; if I tried to jump I'd break my legs.

Then—CRASH!—went the door. Franklin! I looked for a pistol, or a sword, or a fork, or anything I could use to fight him off with, but all I found was Spartacus hiding behind a table—and I didn't think *he* would help me.

There was another crash, and this time the door flew off its hinges and fell to the floor with a bang; the next second here comes Franklin charging in like an angry bull. At the same time I saw a flash of red behind him, but I was too worried about Franklin just then to give it much thought.

He whipped out his pistol and aimed it at my heart.

"Go to the devil, boy!" he thundered.

"You first!" said another voice.

It was Rosie—and before Franklin could turn around she ran up to him and poked her knife into his back. He let out a yell and fell onto his knees; a split second later—BANG!— went his pistol, and I felt a white-hot pain shoot across my arm. The shot scared Spartacus out from behind the table.

"That was for my father," Rosie said.

Then she picked up a logbook and clobbered him over the head with it. The blow staggered him, but didn't knock him down, and before Rosie could take another swing at him he jumped to his feet and knocked her out with his pistol.

Well, that made me so booming mad I forgot I was shot, and I put my head down and charged at him. He happened to be standing in front of the hole just then, and I hit him so hard the two of us went sailing out through it—I should say three of us, because Spartacus was taking shelter behind Franklin, so we took him along with us. He went skidding over the edge with a yelp and dropped straight down into the water, while me and Franklin shot out through the hole together and landed on the floe fifteen feet below. Franklin landed on the floe, I mean; I landed on Franklin.

I rolled off him. He looked dead. That was all right; no one would get any complaints about that from me.

Then I remembered Spartacus. I got up and stumbled to the edge of the floe, where I found him yelping and trying to claw his way onto the ice. I grabbed his collar and hauled him up onto the floe with my good arm. I don't know how I did it; he was a big dog, and after I let go of him I felt so woozy I almost toppled over.

Spartacus shook himself off and gave me a funny kind of look. Then—

"Confound you, boy!" somebody says.

I turned around—and there was Franklin, glaring at me like he was never dead! Before I could budge he had me by the throat. I tried to pry his fingers from my neck, but they were like steel, and the next thing I knew little spots of light were dancing around in front of my eyes.

Then here comes Spartacus flying up out of nowhere and takes *Franklin* by the throat—with his jaws. Down to the ice they went, with Franklin looking positively *confounded* while Spartacus paid him back for every kick and unkind word he had ever received, "with interest," as my grampa would say. I could've watched if I'd wanted to, but I didn't want to.

About that time a cheer broke out from the decks of the *Terror*, and when I looked up to see what it was about there was the professor, and Captain McClintock, and Baldy and a few other Sea Leopards, and Dr. Little and Mr. Honey, all standing along the rail, pointing and cheering. Why are they cheering, I wondered? And what are they pointing at?

Then I saw it. There was a ship steaming out of the fog— a modern ship, with a high, graceful bow.

It was the *Sea Leopard*.

CHAPTER 36

HOME AGAIN

PROFESSOR Meriwether sent Awkward down to the ice floe to get Spartacus and me, and then Captain Crump brought the *Sea Leopard* alongside the *Terror* and came aboard. All the Sea Leopards—the ones who were still alive, anyway—crowded around him, and shook his hand, and laughed and were so glad to see him that they forgot to call him "sir." Of course we wanted to know how he came to be in the Devil's Graveyard and not at the bottom of the sea like we thought he was, but he just ran his stern black eyes over the scene of the battle, and said there'd be time for catching up once the wounded were cared for and the dead buried.

That turned out to be a big job. Of the sixty-six men who had sailed with Franklin, only seventeen were still standing. Before the battle had even begun thirty-six men were buried in the avalanche that thundered down off the iceberg. That was lucky for us, because it evened up the odds considerably, but it wasn't lucky for them. Thirteen others had fallen during the battle, including Franklin and Colonel Gore, and of those just six were still breathing. Dr. Little did all he could for them, but their injuries were so horrible that all but two of them died. On our side only Mr. Honey came through the battle without a scratch. Mr. Pilkington and Mr. Brown had both been killed. So had George Sullivan, I'm sorry to say. He killed those three dragoons who were ganged up on Dr. Little, then when he turned to leave one of the ones he killed shot him in the back and killed *him*. Two Sea Leopards lost their lives, too. Cam Hoffer got run through at the beginning of the battle, and Mr. Clark was done in toward the end. He would never polish his head again.

The *Terror* was already beginning to settle in the water, so all the dead and wounded were moved across to the *Erebus*. Rosie and me went to the sick bay with the other wounded. When my turn came Dr. Little looked at my arm and said I was lucky; it seemed the ball from Franklin's pistol had only just grazed me. So I was never really shot at all. I was awful disappointed. Rosie had an ugly lump on her forehead and a headache, but otherwise she was all right. She stayed in the sick bay for the rest of that morning and afternoon, helping Dr. Little with the wounded; all that blood and gore didn't seem to bother her a bit. I would've stayed and helped, too, but I thought Baldy might need me in the galley.

After the wounded were cared for we sewed up the dead

in canvas bags and laid them out on the deck in a row; then Captain Crump put on his black Sunday coat and read from his old dog-eared Bible, just like his ancestors had done in the days of the clipper ships. When he was done we put the dead on a board, one by one, and tipped them over the side. I cried a little when we slid George over; I won't forget him for as long as I live. We buried all the dead except Franklin, because the ice floe his body was lying on had drifted away, and nobody felt like going out into the fog to look for it.

It was starting to get dark by that time, so we cut away the *Erebus*'s foremast and the *Sea Leopard* towed her out of the Devil's Graveyard. I was glad to leave that awful place, where I'd seen and heard so many horrible things, and get back out into the open again, where I could see the stars, and feel the wind on my face and drink in the cool night air.

The *Terror* we left behind; by that time she had settled so low in the water that the waves were beginning to wash over her quarterdeck. Captain Crump didn't think she'd last out the night. I was glad, for I never wanted to see her again.

That night the captain invited Dr. Little and Mr. Honey to have dinner with him aboard the *Sea Leopard*, along with the professor and Mr. McClintock (he was back to plain old Mr. McClintock now that Captain Crump was back). Rosie and me got invited, too. So did Peerless; the professor was too much of a gentleman to hold a grudge. After dinner the captain went over to his special cabinet and got out a bottle of brandy and a box of cigars, and we all drank brandy and smoked and talked. Except me and Rosie just talked.

First Captain Crump explained how the *Sea Leopard* came to be in the Devil's Graveyard and not sunk by the iceberg like we all thought she'd been. It turned out that just as the *Sea Leopard* was about to roll over, the iceberg ran aground on an underwater shelf that stuck out from the island. The next day the blizzard broke up the pack and swept it out to sea, taking the ship with it. Captain Crump spent the next few days repairing the rudder, which the ice had damaged, and then he steamed back to the island and cruised up and down the coast, trying to contact us on the radio. When he couldn't reach us after three days he decided to steam up to Cape Deception and wait for us there. He figured it would take us about two weeks to hike across the island, but when almost a month went by without any sign of us he decided to head back to Halifax and organize a search. He was steaming past the Devil's Graveyard when he heard what he thought sounded like cannon fire coming out of the fog. It surprised him a good deal, he said, and when he steamed into the fog to investigate and found two tall ships locked in a good old-fashioned sea battle it surprised him even more. He wasn't the only one to be surprised; when Franklin's men saw the *Sea Leopard* looming out of the fog it took all the fight out of them, and they dropped their weapons and surrendered. The entire battle had lasted only six minutes.

Then we told him our story. You already know it, so I'll just say that when Captain Crump heard how we rammed and boarded the *Terror* he smiled for the first time in thirty years. Peerless said he'd personally killed six men during the battle, but nobody believed him, and later on Baldy told me he saw him sneaking onto the *Terror* after the battle was over and picking up a bloody sword.

By that time it was getting late, so we said our good-byes. Dr. Little shook my hand, and said I was a very brave young man and he hoped he'd see me again some day. Then Rosie shook my hand, and said she hoped *she'd* see me again some day, too. I was pretty surprised, because I'd thought she was coming with us.

"I changed my mind," she said. "Dr. Little says everything will be different now that Franklin's gone. He said everyone will get their rights back, and nobody will be sent down to the mines ever again. He said I can live with him and Mrs. Jopson, and he'll teach me how to be a doctor when I'm a little older. I'll be the first girl doctor in New London!"

I tried to get Spartacus to go back to the *Erebus* with Dr. Little and Rosie, but he wouldn't go. He hadn't left my side since the battle; I think he'd decided to adopt me. So I asked Professor Meriwether if we could bring him back to Halifax with us. The professor laughed and said all right.

I won't say too much about the voyage home. We ran into some heavy weather in Melville Sound, and a week later we got trapped in the ice for nine days just south of Cornwallis Island. But after everything we'd just been through, nobody seemed to mind all that much.

We steamed into Halifax Harbour on a drizzly afternoon on the fifth of December, three months to the day after we had left. Peerless was the first one off the ship; he stopped at the top of the gangway just long enough to grind his cigar into the deck and tell Professor Meriwether that he was going to sue him for the loss of his rifle. I don't know if he ever did, but I'm pretty sure the professor won't be inviting him on another expedition anytime soon.

My grampa was waiting for me and Spartacus at the foot of the gangway. He said he'd never worried about me, even after the Coast Guard called to tell him we'd abandoned the *Sea Leopard*; he said he knew Professor Meriwether would keep me safe. Anyhow, he said, he was glad to have me back home, and he hoped I didn't forget to have a good time.

The other day a letter came for me from Mrs. Jopson, of all people. It rambled on for about seventeen pages and was mainly about Mrs. Hornby and the other ladies in her little group of ladies. But among all the tittle-tattle she let it drop that they had a new government up there, and the first thing this new government did was to close the mines. The second was to fire the warden; only then they felt sorry for him, so they gave him a job as a messenger boy. On top of that they made Mr. Honey the new chief judge—and the first thing *he* did was to fire Shanks and move into his office. As for Rosie, Mrs. Jopson had decided to adopt her because she never had any children of her own, while Mrs. Darlington—that's her sister—had seven. She also wrote that Rosie says "Hi," and that she hoped she might be able to bring her down to visit me next year. The letter didn't say anything about the king, or Javelin, or Glim, or any of the other flimps, but I had a feeling they were doing just fine.

CHAPTER 36

I still have nightmares about "the Terror," only instead of it being a cold fog or a creature with no mouth it's Franklin who's chasing me. Some nights I'll wake up all of a sudden, in a cold sweat, and wonder if the whole adventure had just been one long, horrible nightmare. But then I'll hear a sigh from the foot of my bed, and I'll peep over the covers to see two yellow eyes gleaming back at me out of the darkness.

THE END

AFTERWORD

ON MAY 19, 1845, an expedition led by Rear Admiral Sir John Franklin set sail from Greenhithe, England with a crew of 110 sailors and 24 officers. Their mission was to find the legendary Northwest Passage. Among those who sailed with Franklin were Henry Collins, second master; Graham Gore, lieutenant; William Fowler, purser's steward; William Gibson, officers' steward; John Downing, quartermaster; Edward Little, lieutenant; Thomas Jopson, captain's steward; Thomas Darlington, caulker; Frederick John Hornby, mate; Thomas Honey, carpenter; William Shanks, able seaman; John Diggle, cook; William Pilkington, private; Samuel Brown, boatswain's mate; Thomas Blanky, ice master; John Sullivan, captain of the maintop; David Sims, able seaman; Joseph Andrews, captain of the hold; and Joseph Geater, able seaman. Two years later the entire expedition, along with Her Majesty's frigates *Erebus* and *Terror*, vanished in the Canadian Arctic.

CPSIA information can be obtained at www.ICGtesting.com
Printed in the USA
LVOW06s1111211214

419822LV00007B/902/P